Dark Tales of Asi
Cursed Legends and Dark Myths

Delve into the shadows of Asia, where folklore whispers of ancient curses and dark myths chill the soul. In Dark Tales of Asia: 8 Stories of Cursed Legends and Dark Myths, experience the terror that lurks in the corners of forgotten villages and haunted landscapes. From the blood-soaked legends of the Tiyanak to the evil spirit of Aka Manto, each tale weaves a haunting narrative that unravels the mysteries of love, betrayal, and vengeance. These are not just stories; they are warnings that echo through the ages, reminding us that some legends refuse to fade into obscurity. Are you brave enough to turn the pages?

Legends breathe—and they hunger for your fear.

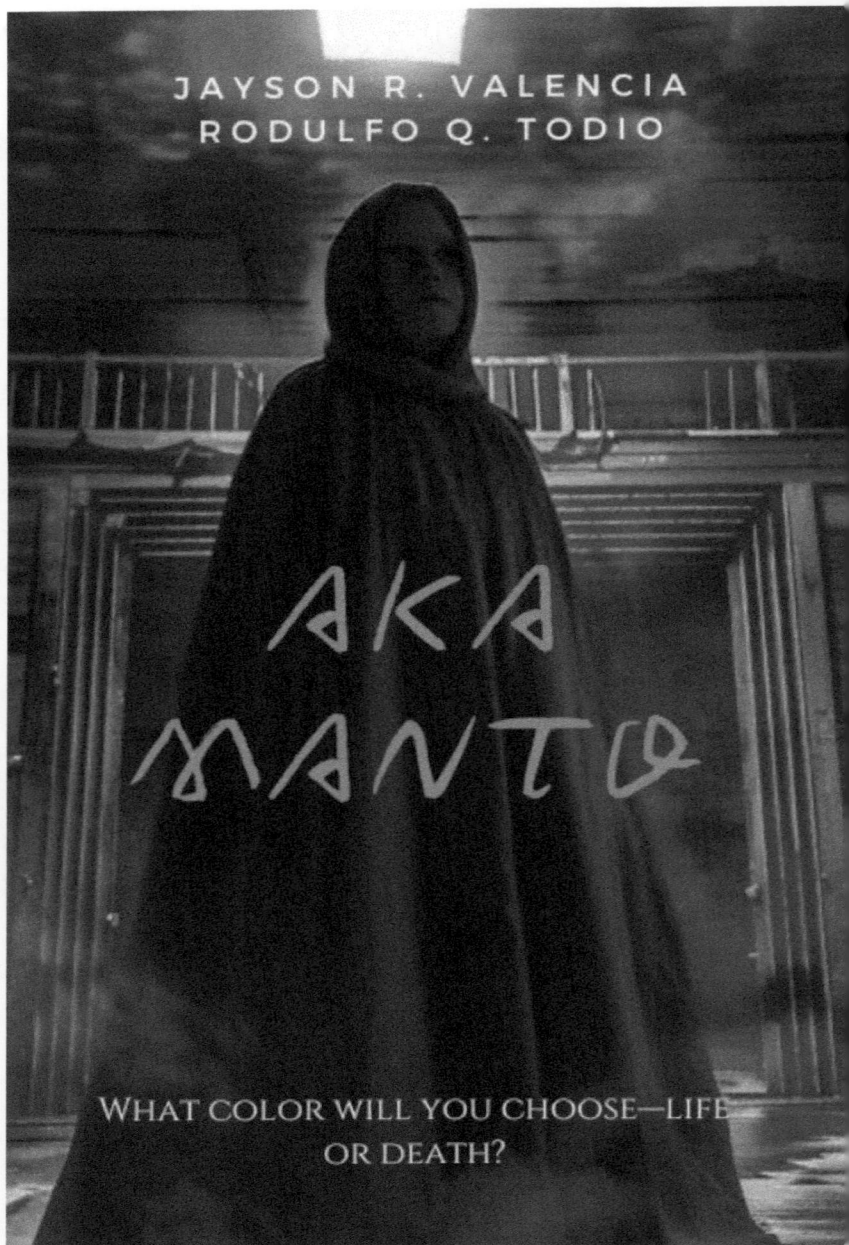

JAYSON R. VALENCIA
RODULFO Q. TODIO

AKA
MANTO

WHAT COLOR WILL YOU CHOOSE—LIFE
OR DEATH?

JAYSON R. VALENCIA
RODULFO Q. TODIO

Dark Tales of Asia

8 Stories of Cursed Legends and Dark Myths

Legends breathe—and they hunger for your fear.

This is a work of fiction. Similarities to real people, places, or events are entirely coincidental.

DARK TALES OF ASIA

First edition. October 8, 2024.

ISBN: 979-8227229274

Written by Jayson Valencia and Rodulfo Todio.

Also by Jayson Valencia

Tales of Haunted Japan: Seven Tales of Horror and the Supernatural
Tales of Filipino Terror: Ten Stories of Myth and Fear
Dark Tales of Asia

Also by Rodulfo Todio

Tales of Haunted Japan: Seven Tales of Horror and the Supernatural
Tales of Filipino Terror: Ten Stories of Myth and Fear
Dark Tales of Asia

Aka Manto

In the heart of Tokyo School of Arts, a seemingly innocent school fair spirals into horror when authorities discover two students brutally murdered in a makeshift haunted restroom booth. Junior high student Motokatsu awakens on a stretcher and finds himself embroiled in a chilling mystery that intertwines urban legend with the darkest corners of human despair. As he delves deeper into the events leading up to the gruesome deaths of his friends, he unravels a truth far more sinister than he ever imagined. With suspicion clouding his mind and an evil spirit haunting the school, Motokatsu must confront Aka Manto and the shadows of his friendships.
What color will you choose—life or death?

Introduction

The smell of blood, feces, and urine permeates the air. The smell was so strong that it woke me up. Everything was hazy. I remembered running after I opened the last cubicle, tripping on my shoelace, and hitting my head on the wall. I don't know anything else after that. I slowly touched my head and saw fresh blood trickling from the bruise. I must have blacked out after I hit the wall.

I scanned the room and saw Michio standing in front of the last cubicle, holding a bloodied knife in his hand. He was just standing there and looking inside as if in a trance.

"Michio," I called.

I saw him twitch when he heard his name. He screamed while looking inside the cubicle. He fell to the floor and immediately crawled away from the cubicle after he landed, dropping the knife in the process. As soon as he saw his bloodied hands, he screamed again and cried.

"What happened, Michio? What happened?" I carefully stood up while still holding my head. I was dizzy and had to hold onto the wall as I stood. I looked at Michio again, who was now crouching in a fetal position beside the wall.

I slowly worked my way to the last cubicle, holding the wall with my left hand while my right hand was holding my bloodied head. I vomited as soon as I saw what Michio saw inside the cubicle.

There was blood splattered everywhere. Toshiro's head was shoved down onto the toilet bowl, and he was drowned in his blood and urine. He had multiple stab wounds on his back. My eyes widened when I saw this, and I looked at Michio and the knife that fell from his bloodied hands. As if on instinct, I backed away from him.

"I didn't do it, I didn't, " Michio said.

I lost my balance and crashed into the next cubicle where Toshiro's dead body was. To my horror, our other group member, Satoshi, sat on the bowl. He was not breathing, his skin was all blue, and he had dark marks on his neck. Satoshi fell from the toilet bowl on top of me. He was stiff and heavy. I almost choked when I vomited again. I don't remember anything else after that because I must have blacked out again.

Act 1: A Bloody School Fair

I woke up on a stretcher, sprawled on the toilet floor. Michio, who was also on a stretcher with his hands and legs restrained, was next to me. The paramedics are in the process of moving Satoshi's body away from the room. I could see a massive crowd of students and teachers outside of the door behind the police line. There were a lot of police in their blue and white uniforms coming and going. They cordoned off the crime scene with police tape. Some are pushing nosy students away from the vicinity.

The smell of blood still filled the entire restroom. I looked at the first cubicle and saw that, from my location, Toshiro's head was still stuck in the toilet bowl despite several firefighters' efforts to pull him out.

The paramedics carried Michio and me to the ambulance, passing the students gathered outside the cordoned school restroom. I could see their curiosity about what had happened. Contempt filled their eyes as they brought me out of the restroom. "My God, they think we killed Toshiro and Satoshi," I whispered to myself.

Later, I heard from the nurses that the firemen took almost an hour to remove Toshiro's head from the bowl. They mentioned that his head seemed pulled or dragged onto the toilet bowl. Satoshi, on the other hand, died of asphyxiation. Someone choked him in such a rage that the bones in his neck snapped. Both of them died gruesomely.

I am a junior high school student at the Tokyo School of Arts. Our school's cultural festival should have been fun but wasn't enjoyable. Our group decided to create a haunted horror booth for the event. We used our utmost creativity. We had no desire to harm anyone. After observing the students' hostile looks, I stared at the school grounds. There was a fire truck, an ambulance, and a police car with loud sirens on the school grounds.

We are group 4, a group of not-so-bright students. Toshiro, Satoshi, Michio, and my name is Motokatsu. Toshiro and Satoshi are dead, while Michio and I are the prime suspects behind the killing. I need to know what happened.

Act 2: Michio's Account and Revelation

After our medical checkup, Michio and I were brought to a small room with mirrors on one side of the wall. We were left there for an hour without anyone checking on us. I noticed the CCTV hanging on the ceiling on top of the mirror. Michio and I were both silent during that time. After a while, I finally decided to ask some questions.

"Michio, what happened?" I looked at him intently. He was avoiding my eyes, and his whole body was shaking. After what seemed like a minute, he calmed his nerves and was about to speak when the door opened.

It was the investigator of the case. He introduced himself as Officer Saito. He sat in one of the empty chairs beside Michio. He looked at both of us and tapped Michio on the shoulder. "You were about to tell Motokatsu something. Start at the beginning," he prompted, dropping his audio recorder on the table.

Michio expressed his desire to go home. "I want to go home."

"Then tell me the truth so we can catch the culprit and set you free," the cop convinced him softly.

I realized that he was establishing rapport and using his skills in investigating. I looked at Michio, who was looking at the ceiling and shaking his head.

"I did not kill Toshiro nor Satoshi." He held his head with his right arm. "They told us we had the worst idea for this school fair."

"Your group converted the restroom into a horror booth and made the terror real, right?" the cop asked.

"Our homeroom teacher told us to present Japanese culture or folklore," Michio protested. He looked at me and pointed his finger. "It was his idea to summon the Aka Manto. So, I did."

"You summoned the Aka Manto?" I was shocked. "Why did you do that?"

"The other groups were insulting us," Michio confessed. "They told me we don't belong in the School of Arts."

"Hey, what is this, Aka Manto?" the investigator asked.

"Aka Manto inspired our school fair design. It is a Japanese urban legend about a spirit who appears to individuals using restrooms in public or school restrooms. It is masked and dressed in a red cloak," Michio answered.

"We saw some red cloaks in your booth's entrance," the cop said, touching his chin with two fingers.

I admitted, "I came up with the idea to dress up and act out the legend. We ask anyone who pays and enters our restroom booth to use the toilet in the last stall; then, we ask if they prefer red or blue toilet paper."

The police investigator narrowed his eyes by bringing together his eyelids, showing an expression of doubt or contempt. But he smiled and asked, "What if one answers blue?"

"The Aka Manto will strangle him until he becomes suffocated and turns blue." Michio quickly answered.

"However, we devised that by spraying blue paint on those who chose blue and red paint on those who chose red," I added.

The investigator tilted his head and raised his eyebrows. The officer wrinkled his forehead. "So Satoshi selected blue toilet paper?" Then he shouted, "Why is Toshiro's fucking head stuck in the toilet?"

"He chose not to answer," Michio responded emotionlessly.

"What? Is this a joke to you?" The cop stood up, his mouth pulled away to one side. His eyes were also looking sideways and upward. His phone vibrated, and he got a message from his research team about the legend of Aka Manto. He sat down and read it silently. Then he murmured, "What the heck is going on?"

Act 3: I Remember Now

Our hospital arrest has been causing us a lot of stress. I looked at Michio and remembered the times he was mocked by my classmates and other schoolmates whenever he performed on the stage. Almost everyone downplayed his talent in theater, so he settled into a background production. However, people ridiculed him even though he had theatrical backdrops. It could be the main reason why he summoned the Aka Manto.

He was successful this time. The horror booth turned into reality. The spirit with a red cape appeared; the Aka Manto was real.

Michio started talking again. "Motokatsu tasked Satoshi and Toshiro to spray paint on the students who entered our horror booth while we were both assigned to the entrance to collect fees."

He was right. I recalled two students coming out of the restroom booth, smiling after being sprayed with blue and red paint on their hair. We felt satisfied. Michio gave me a high five. Then, some minutes later, Satoshi came out of the booth and mentioned a bad smell inside the restroom.

Toshiro had a sour stomach and was defecating. The smell was so strong that we temporarily closed the booth entrance. Satoshi had a sour stomach, too, after a few minutes. He tried to find another restroom, but someone occupied the nearest one, and the other was too far away. He covered his nose with his mask and entered the bathroom.

We got curious that the two never came out, so I asked Michio to check on the two. I heard Michio screaming, so I followed him into the restroom. I saw him in the fourth and last cubicle, holding a bloodied knife in his hand. He was standing there and looking inside as if in a trance. Then I saw a floating red cloak, so I ran. My head hit the wall, and I passed out.

Act 4: Michio's Death

Officer Saito was visibly angry when he slammed his fist on the table. He grabbed the audio recorder and clicked pause.

"I am not here to listen to both of your bullshit! Two kids died today, and both of you are suspects," he pushed the table and stood up.

Michio and I were speechless.

"I'm going out of that door. When I come back, you better tell us the real story," The investigator said. He walked to the door and violently nudged it open. We were looking at him when he suddenly stopped and looked back at us. "We're not playing," he warned, but we didn't know what it meant.

As soon as he left the room, the CCTV moved and pointed to our location, and the red LED light below the lens started blinking.

"It's your fault," I said softly.

"What? Don't point your fingers at me! It was your idea to decorate the toilet in the Aka Manto theme," Michio said, pointing to my chest.

"You called out the Aka Manto! Your action killed our friends and probably us too!" I said as I pushed his hands away from me.

At that moment, we heard the sound of a toilet flushing. Our eyes widened when we realized that there was a toilet in our room.

We both looked at the origin of the sound. I could see the cold sweat dripping from Michio's face. My heart, on the other hand, is pounding on overdrive. The light in the room flickered for a moment. That made Michio almost scream out, yet he managed to stifle his mouth. We heard another flush, then another, and another. Whoever is inside the toilet is doing it on purpose. Each flush interval was faster than before until, all of a sudden, it stopped. We kept our eyes on the door. We stood up and started backing away from the toilet.

Michio ran towards the door where Officer Saito had exited. He twisted the handle and pulled the door, but it didn't budge. Someone locked it from the outside. He kept trying.

We held our breath as the door slightly opened. We're bracing ourselves for anything that would go out of that door, but there's none—a minute passed. Two. Three. We looked at each other. Could it be that there was just an earthquake that triggered the flush and opened the door? After all, tremors are frequent in our area.

That was what Michio was thinking because he got cocky and was wearing a wide grin on his face as he started walking to the toilet.

"What? Are you thinking that the Aka Manto would follow us here?" he scoffed with a derogatory laugh.

I smiled sheepishly, thinking those watching the CCTV would laugh at two scared boys. Then suddenly, a woman's voice came from the toilet door.

"What color of toilet paper do you want? Red or blue?" the voice asked, probably to Michio.

Michio peed his pants from fear. We're both aware that if he responds, the Aka Manto will stab him to death. If he answered "blue," the entity would grab his neck and suffocate him. If he didn't answer, the entity would drag him to the toilet bowl like Toshiro's death. Poor Toshiro probably refused to answer at first, but then, as he was about to open his mouth to answer, for some reason, he suddenly stopped. The Aka Manto forcefully dragged him into the toilet bowl.

Michio started crying and held his hands towards me. He didn't manage to ask for help because a dark figure clothed in red and wearing a kabuki mask stormed out of the toilet and grabbed him by the head. I loudly cried when I saw this. I was screaming at the top of my lungs. I could hear Michio's skull cracking. I knew I was next, so I ran towards the door, hoping that I could kick it open. That's when I tripped again from my dangling shoelace. I was moving so fast that I knocked myself out cold when my head hit the door.

The Aka Manto can't ask a question to an unconscious person, which is why I survived him twice.

-The End-

In the heart of Tokyo School of Arts, a seemingly innocent school fair spirals into horror when authorities discover two students brutally murdered in a makeshift haunted restroom booth. Junior high student Motokatsu awakens on a stretcher and finds himself embroiled in a chilling mystery that intertwines urban legend with the darkest corners of human despair. As he delves deeper into the events leading up to the gruesome deaths of his friends, he unravels a truth far more sinister than he ever imagined. With suspicion clouding his mind and an evil spirit haunting the school, Motokatsu must confront Aka Manto and the shadows of his friendships.

Written by
Jayson R. Valencia
Rodulfo Q. Todio

Krasue

Beware the hunger that never dies

JAYSON R. VALENCIA
RODULFO Q. TODIO

Krasue

A couple's dream of parenthood spirals into a nightmare in a coastal village steeped in folklore and shadowed by tragedy. When Lawan, a devoted wife, finds an abandoned girl named Karawek near a mysterious shipping container, she takes her in, unwittingly inviting an evil force into their home. As sinister events unfold, fear grips the village, children vanish, and circumstances tear lives apart, triggering an ancient curse. Will Lawan's love and bravery be enough to confront the horror lurking in the shadows, or will the village succumb to the darkness that feasts on its very soul?
Beware the hunger that never dies.

Prologue

An abandoned shipping container was open and was partially embedded in the sand on the beach as the salty water slammed on its side. Many people had already gathered around it, some pointing to the flag of Thailand painted on the side. When I arrived, the police were already on the scene. I asked one of the policemen what they thought happened, but he just shook his head. Some of the bystanders then started speculating that the shipping container contained elicit goods, perhaps illegal drugs. Some said that it contained illegal immigrants that dispersed when the container opened. None of us knew what had happened. One thing is sure: blood was dripping and mixing into the nearby waters.

Act 1: Lawan

My wife Lawan woke up early as she promised to go to the image of the reclining woman in the Tham Luang Nang-Non cave to offer flowers. She has been married to me for ten years and just got pregnant for the first time after making a devotion to the shrine. The villagers named the shrine after a princess who, according to tradition, committed suicide after they forbade her from being with her commoner love. According to the legend, her body became the mountain, and her genitals became the cave.

"Look! These krachiao flowers that I gathered from the garden are so beautiful; the lady will be pleased!" she smiled as she brandished the flowers in front of me.

"Be careful, Lawan, and come home early," I replied to her as I left for work. But because I felt uneasy and worried about her going alone to the cave, I returned and decided to accompany her first to the Tham Luang Nang-Non Forest Park.

"Thank you, Aat, my love," she lovingly kissed me, thrilled that I would accompany her.

Lawan looked at me with delight as she picked up the Ratchaphruek flower hanging from a tree. I felt happy deep inside because I genuinely love Lawan's jolly outlook on life. We then decided to leave and fulfill her devotion. We arrived at the Forest Park before noon that day. She strolled and approached the image of the reclining woman. She looked at her beautiful face and greeted her with a smile. She lit some incense sticks and put down the flowers she picked from her garden. Shen then closed her eyes and said her prayers. She touched her belly as she remembered being thankful for being pregnant.

I left her then as I needed to leave for work. Before that very day, as we were cuddling in bed, Lawan opened up about her feelings and concerns. She mentioned that she remembered that I almost left her because Lawan wanted to have a child, and she had been having miscarriages in the past. She asked the lady to protect her baby from any harm.

She opened her eyes and was shocked to see the face of the reclining woman staring at her with an evil stare. She was stunned and felt much shaken, so she hurriedly left. Lawan looked at me with tears flowing as if asking what the meaning was. I assured her that it was only a bad dream.

That night, after I got home, Lawan was excited to tell me how her day happened.

She said that during the afternoon, she stopped by the beach on her way home and walked up to a broken-down shipping container. Not far from the abandoned shipping container, she discovered a Thai girl who appeared exhausted and untidy and was eating her feces. She felt pity for the girl. She quickly rinsed her with seawater and gave her a piece of bread that she brought along. The girl did not accept it at first and was visibly confused, but she came nearer, alternating her gaze on Lawan and her pregnant tummy.

"Don't be afraid, I won't harm you," she whispered as she gave the piece of bread.

The girl took the bread and smelled it. When she noticed the piece of meat in it, she devoured it. Lawan smiled at the sight of this and decided to take her home. They came across some policemen investigating the recent events in their place.

Lawan helped the Thai girl take a bath to rinse off the salt and clean the remaining feces from her body. The girl can't talk but can only utter one word: Karawek. For this reason, she called her Karawek. Karawek acted differently as her eyes would look from top to bottom, and she refused to be touched. She would, however, smile when she looked at Lawan's belly. To establish a connection, Lawan allowed the girl to touch her bulging belly. She is eight months pregnant and already has a large belly.

"Do you have a family?" Lawan asked.

Karawek shook her head and stared at Lawan. Lawan felt uneasy and scared. She can't explain the feeling; it is the same fright you would feel if you were staring at a poisonous snake ready to strike at any time. She shook off the feeling and backed off a few meters, pretending to fix the sofa. She quickly came back when she gathered enough courage.

"Let me be your mother, and that's our baby." Lawan pointed to the baby in her womb.

Karawek smiled and walked towards Lawan, then touched her belly once again.

"I... I like... hungry," Karawek's eyes glared. Lawan told me it was the first time she had noticed that Karawek had a vast and booming eye.

When I arrived home, I saw my wife falling asleep while Kawaek touched her belly.

I was surprised to see Karawek touching my wife in the belly while she was sleeping in a rocking chair. Karawek was sitting on the floor, and her head was close to my wife's belly like a young girl embracing her mother. Lawan woke up and explained to me how she had found Karawek. She pleaded with me to let her stay in the house.

"Please let her stay," she pleaded. "Her name is Karawek."

I saw Karawek showing signs of asking for pity in the corner of the room. I was convinced and let Karawek stay in one of our rooms. However, I had some hesitations about this decision. I looked for something in my toolbox under the bed. I nodded when I found it.

Act 2: Eaten

That evening, I overheard creaking and thudding noises outside our room's window and door that sounded like someone was trying to break in. When we arrived, Lawan and I went to Karawek's room but discovered the girl was gone. As I searched the area for intruders and looked for our missing guest, I instructed my wife to lock herself in our room. My wife became worried about Karawek, but it was almost midnight, and she felt some discomfort in her stomach. She agreed to just stay in bed with me.

"Where is she?" I asked myself. I had some suspicion, but I didn't want to upset my wife, so I locked our room and lay in the bed beside her. I could not sleep that night as I remembered what had happened on the beach. I promised myself that I would protect my wife against any harm.

Then I heard high-pitched noises and swooshing sounds coming from outside. I left the house to investigate the cause of the noise. When I got close to the cluster of banana trees, I discovered a headless body there. I woke up from the nightmare and looked at my wife, who lay covered in blood with her belly ripped open. I shouted, and she jolted me awake.

"You are having a nightmare!" Lawan worriedly mentioned.

I looked at her belly and embraced her. I heard the sound of roosters, indicating it was already morning. But that morning, I was greeted by the wailing cry of a mother who found her 3-year-old son dead and half-eaten in his room. It seemed that a dangerous animal devoured the boy and feasted on his internal organs.

The news spread so fast that I told Lawan to be careful. My wife was worried about why Karawek was not in the room, so we looked for her. We later found the Thai girl wandering in our neighborhood.

"Karawek, where were you last night?" Lawan worriedly asked.

Lawan embraced her and guided her back home. I wanted to disagree, but I had no choice as I saw how my wife loved Karawek. I looked at Karawek, and she smiled at me innocently. That smile captured my heart, but I still had some doubts.

Act 3: Darkness

I noticed the Thai girl looking suspiciously on several occasions at my wife's pregnant belly. She can't contain herself and would always be around Lawan. I told my wife about my worries, but she laughed. To avoid an argument, we dismissed the concern as a typical fascination of someone on seeing a pregnant woman.

I also felt biased against Karawek, who was not a teenager yet. She was innocent and couldn't be part of what I suspected because she was too small, frail, and innocent.

That night, I volunteered to join the neighborhood watch to help find the culprit that killed our neighbor's son. It proved fatal for my wife. We roamed around the town and even went to the mountain's base but did not hear or see anything. We decided to go back home. Then, as I approached, I listened to the same high-pitched and swooshing sound in our house. Creaking and thudding sounds followed it. I opened the door and went to our room, but I was shocked by what I saw. I found Lawan dead, dripping in her blood. Someone opened her womb, and they ate the baby. I cried out loud, embracing my wife.

Then, I stood up and looked for Karawek, but the Thai girl was missing from her room again. I was sure at that point that she was the monster responsible for terrorizing our neighborhood.

Act 4: Hunt for the Missing Guest

When I left the house, I was shocked to see that someone had discovered several kids and farm animals dead.

One of my neighbors yelled at me, "Your wife brought us this curse."

"Yes, she brought that Thai girl to our town!" another neighbor shouted.

"There were already some incidents of the Krause haunting this town even before Karawek came to our house!" I answered them. "I also lost my wife, and I will do everything to avenge her!"

We decided to unite to make tools like bamboo spears and sharp knives; some even brought rifles to catch the culprit. The whole town is now in a frenzy to find the Thai girl they think was doing all this.

"We may need to search the forest in the mountain!" I suggested.

"Yes, let us build some traps," the sheriff ordered. "We can't afford to lose another life."

That day, we went to the forest and built enormous traps. Some built noose traps to catch the culprit. Some created many deadfall traps using logs. I also built a rope swing trap tied to a tree. It releases a wrecking ball of stone that may instantly kill anyone who touches or triggers it. We were confident that we could catch Karawek this time.

Act 5: The Hunger of Krasue

As we returned home, the village loudly sobbed when night came. The Krause slaughtered every pregnant woman, leaving their belly exposed. Someone consumed their embryos. One thing is apparent to those who saw them die: a woman's floating head did it! It has a floating head that glows, and its internal organs hang from the neck and trail after the head.

The sheriff shook his head and recalled an episode from his youth. He said a hungry old lady had arrived in this town and asked for food. There was famine, and everyone was poor, resulting from mega typhoons that destroyed farmlands.

The sheriff said, "Everyone was hungry and had no food, so no one helped that old woman. That woman swore at our town and said she would return."

I argued, "But it's unfair that we are paying for the past's mistakes."

"Everyone was starving at the time, so you shouldn't hold the people responsible," the sheriff responded.

"Evildoers frequently point the finger at others for their actions, yet they bear the responsibility. Let us protect our town!" I declared. "Let us bring justice to the victims!"

Act 6: The Death of Krasue

That night, we roamed around our village with our torches while we let some men stay with the women who conducted a mass funeral for all the victims. We carried knives, spears, and rifles as our weapons. Then, I heard the same high-pitched and swooshing noise from the clustered banana leaves. I noticed that the cluster of banana trees looked the same as my nightmare, and when I looked closer, I saw the headless body of the Krause.

"It's here," I shouted. I can't be mistaken. That's Karawek's body; the shirt that she was wearing was what my wife gave her. I was in so much rage at that point.

We pierced the headless body of the Krause with our bamboo spears and knives and burned it with our torches. We felt a particular accomplishment while doing it, but suddenly, the Krause appeared. Her head twisted with anger and evil intent as she tried to wrap us with her long tongue.

Using his rifle, the sheriff fired a couple of shots, but the Krause was not hurt. Her tongue tried to reach him, and since I was close, I reached out for my knife and cut her tongue. The Krause grimaced in pain. It flew away, and we tried following it.

We kept following until the early rays of the dawn came and destroyed the Krause. Our mourning turned into a celebration. We killed the Krause. Our town is free!

We celebrated while mourning for our dead. Some elderly men believed we should delay the celebration out of respect for the dead, but the sheriff disagreed and told us we would waste the dead animals if we didn't cook them. Most people complied with the authority of the sheriff and cooked the dead and injured animals like cows and pigs, which the Krause attacked.

There was a considerable merry-making that night. Men drank alcoholic drinks and devoured the food as if there was no tomorrow.

Unhappy with the celebration, an elderly man shook his head and yelled that it was an abomination to the dead.

The sheriff stood up and shouted, "Shut up! It's time to celebrate. We killed the monster!"

Epilogue

Locals started exhibiting the same behavior as the Thai girl when they ate the injured and half-eaten animals. I swear I even saw some of their eyes become unusually large. It was fortunate for me that I loved Lawan so much that I did not celebrate with them. I hurriedly left the place and moved to Myanmar.

-The End-

A couple's dream of parenthood spirals into a nightmare in a coastal village steeped in folklore and shadowed by tragedy. When Lawan, a devoted wife, finds an abandoned girl named Karawek near a mysterious shipping container, she takes her in, unwittingly inviting an evil force into their home. As sinister events unfold, fear grips the village, children vanish, and circumstances tear lives apart, triggering an ancient curse. Will Lawan's love and bravery be enough to confront the horror lurking in the shadows, or will the village succumb to the darkness that feasts on its very soul?

Written by
Jayson R. Valencia
Rodulfo Q. Todio

JAYSON R. VALENCIA
RODULFO Q. TODIO

YUKI-ONNA

SNOW FALLS, LIVES FREEZE, TERROR AWAKENS.

Yuki-Onna

In the heart of a snow-cloaked mountain, four friends embark on what should be a fun-filled winter getaway at Zao Onsen Ski Resort. But when a fierce snowstorm traps them in their cabin, they find themselves haunted by a chilling presence: the Yuki-Onna, a ghostly figure from Japanese folklore known for her beauty and deadly allure. Ultimately, circumstances test their friendship when Yuka confronts the chilling reality of survival amidst betrayal and haunting loss as terror unfolds.

Snow falls, lives freeze, and terror awakens.

Introduction

I, Yuka Nakamura, along with my friends Haruka Tanaka, Taro Suzuki, and Satoshi Yamamoto, had decided to spend our winter vacation at a remote mountain ski resort called Zao Onsen, located in Yamagata prefecture, which is known for its "snow monsters." Heavy snow and ice cover these trees and tall shrubs, which look like snow monsters, hence the name. Winter sports enthusiasts love the Zao Onsen Ski Resort because of its hot springs and traditional Japanese-style lodging. The resort appeared deserted when we arrived, and heavy snowfall was outside. We seemed to be the only people there due to the intense weather. I couldn't get rid of the impression that someone was keeping an eye on us. I dismissed it and explained that we had already experienced tension during the resort trip.

The resort was nestled high in the snowy peaks, surrounded by dense forests and pristine white snow. The ski chalet where we stayed was a large wooden cabin with a warm and cozy interior, but as soon as we stepped outside, the cold and isolation made us feel as if we were the only ones there, and indeed, there was no one else in the resort. We speculated that everyone left because of the impending snowstorm. The chill wind that bit at our skin added to the eerie atmosphere and the sense of foreboding.

My best friend Haruka, a 25-year-old recent graduate working as a trainee at a marketing company, dropped her gears and walked towards me with a worried expression. She smiled timidly, and I could sense her unease in the eerie atmosphere. I understood how she felt, as the isolation also made me uneasy. Haruka is hardworking and ambitious, with a keen sense of business acumen and a creative side expressed through painting and photography. I convinced her to come on this trip to paint the snow-covered trees the resort is known for.

Taro, a 23-year-old university student studying engineering, is practical, logical, and never panics. He quickly inspected our cabin, declared it safe, and suggested we wait out the storm and enjoy free accommodation. Though he was trying to find a solution and stay positive, the unease in the atmosphere was affecting even him, as I could see in his eyes. Taro is an outdoors enthusiast who enjoys hiking and skiing. I met him at the university, and we've been friends since.

Satoshi, a 27-year-old recent graduate working as a software developer, is adventurous, outgoing, and always looking for thrills. He stayed outside, scanning the area for a spot to explore. He entered the cabin after a few minutes, and his expression showed that he, too, was feeling the eerie atmosphere and isolation. Satoshi is quiet and reserved, brilliant, and skilled in programming. He is also a close friend of Haruka; they met in the university photography club and still collaborate on projects.

As we settled in, we couldn't shake off the feeling that something was wrong. The mood was unease and foreboding, as we didn't know what would happen next.

Act 1: Early Encounter

Despite the increasingly severe weather, we decided to trek the following day. Regardless, we didn't hear any weather-related warnings. In addition, extreme activities like skiing and snowboarding are better off being dangerous.

Harsh Siberian winds carve spooky humanoid shapes out of snow-covered trees in Mount Zao each winter. From the translucent window glass in the room, I could see that the snow had blanketed the trees, creating monster-like shapes that appeared to obstruct anyone's path. They looked alive and moving. Various names for the mysterious frozen phenomenon appear atop Japan's Mount Zao, including Juhyou, snow, and ice monsters. Whatever name it goes by, this slope of ice sculptures is a mysterious sight.

Simply put, it was a mysterious snowy mountain. When a breeze stirs the air, the newly fallen snow bounces on top of the hardened snow, glistening with ice crystals. I have visited that location numerous times, but for the first time, I felt something was wrong. I stayed because I wanted to be with my friends. We rode in a snow truck to get around the mountain's base and view the sights. Haruka and Satoshi quickly took photographs of the landscape. Upon looking at the pictures in their gallery, these snow monsters seemed to be staring at us.

I got out of the vehicle and looked at the place. Tiny snowflakes fell onto the ground from the sky's grey, puffy clouds. I froze as I stood there. When the chilly wind blew, a river of snot burst out of my nose. The viscous snot had severely obstructed my ability to smell. The cold stream seeped through my boots to my silky socks, numbing my feet. My feet had the sensation of having stepped into an icy ocean. I felt like I had fallen through the ice and was stranded there. For a brief moment, I resembled a lost thrall as I stood outside for the first time in a very long time, soaking in the sights, sounds, and everything else that came

with being outside. I felt again the snow beneath me chewing my feet
and the brisk wind brushing over my body. Around my black rubber
boot, the sizable mound of ice-white snow feels almost like quicksand.

Taro got out of the truck and laughed when he saw me. Satoshi
also left the vehicle, leaving his camera on his chest. He assisted me by
pulling me out off the ground and asking if I was okay. He also lent me
his handkerchief.

"He was a real gentleman," I told myself. "Thank you," I murmured
as I bowed down.

As we approached the snow mountain's base, trees surrounded us
and reflected a few spooky apparitions. The snow hushed the
landscape. Our snow truck hovered only a few feet above the ground
and returned to our cabin.

A lone elderly guest attendant met us and gave me a weird vibe. I
guess she came back to the resort when we were hiking. She gave us
the itineraries and keys. We headed to our room dressed in our ski and
snowboarding safety gear. We spent some time in front of the fireplace
to keep warm. My body trembled, and my teeth chattered from the
cold. I clenched and unclenched my hurting fingers to keep feeling
in their tips. My toes and earlobes were burning, and I heard some
eerie whisper telling me something I couldn't grasp. I was dazed and
confused when Taro knocked on my door to tell me they were prepared
to return for another ride. He joined Haruka and Satoshi, who wore ski
attire.

Despite having reservations because I had a bad feeling about this
ride, I found myself nodding.

We left the cabin and drove to the higher mountain region using
the snow vehicle we had rented from the resort. Even though it was
not my first time, I still felt anxious. I picture the snow-covered trees
forming the shapes of cryptids or humanoids waiting to devour us.

We were laughing when Taro and I suddenly froze because we
noticed something staring at us from afar. My heart was pounding in

my chest as I realized that we were not alone. "Someone was watching us," I pointed to the figure.

"I noticed that too," Taro pointed his finger as well. "There."

Out of the shadows stepped a woman, her inhumanly beautiful face twisted into an ominous expression. She stared at us with her cold, lifeless eyes, and I could feel the chill of her gaze penetrating the very core of my being. Her long black hair and blue lips stood out against the white snow, and a gust of cold wind accompanied her presence and made my skin crawl.

As she slowly advanced towards us, fear paralyzed us. Her ghostly form floated across the snow as her eyes locked on us. We panicked and quickly got to the vehicle.

Satoshi asked us in the driver's seat, "Did you see the woman floating toward us?"

Adrenaline flooded my body at a lightning-fast rate, and I was amazed and afraid at the same time.

Act 2: Trapped and Tormented

The snowstorm worsened as we drove back to the ski chalet, making it difficult to see the road ahead. A blizzard made the visibility almost zero. Suddenly, our speeding snow vehicle bumped into a tree, causing the car to spin out of control. The vehicle threw us around inside, and the impact caused minor injuries to all of us. We were trapped inside the car, unable to move, as the severe snowstorm raged outside. We quickly realized that we were stranded, with no way to contact for help and no way to escape. The blizzard was worsening, and we knew we had to act fast to survive.

I looked down at the window. There was movement. It was about the size of a tall woman, and she was skinny. She was pale and had what looked to be a head of straight, white hair. Its gait was jerky like someone making a bad attempt at dancing. Legs came first, then hips, then the torso, then the shoulders, then the neck, and finally the head. It appeared to be gazing at me, in my opinion. I experienced prickliness throughout. I didn't know what it was. I initially believed it to be a heron or some other type of bird, but it was far too human-like. However, it didn't move as a person would.

With its face still directed at me, it moved away from my direction. It's like a beehive that I poked. Before entering the iced-covered trees, it made that strange, jerking movement with its body. I tried to watch the field as it passed, but the snow-covered bamboo stalks remained perfectly still. I noticed that the snow did not have any foot marks on them. After a while, it suddenly vanished. So I took the time to make sure that every one of us was alright.

When we finally managed to free ourselves from being pinned down, I told them what I saw, and they looked at each other, saying Haruka has the same experience. While talking, we saw a towering figure looking at us in the window. It was about six feet tall. We saw a tall, beautiful woman with long black hair and blue lips. Her inhumanly pale or even transparent skin made her blend into the snowy landscape. She wore a white kimono. Despite her inhuman beauty, her eyes strike terror.

Not long after, we all felt an overwhelming sense of sleepiness. We thought it was just the adrenaline wearing off, so we tried to fight it but eventually fell asleep. But when I woke up, an ice-cold breeze and snow rushed inside the vehicle's open door to greet me. I immediately realized that something was wrong. Satoshi, our adventurous friend, was not inside the car. We searched for him using a flashlight, but what we found was too gruesome to describe.

Ice covered Satoshi's body, and someone drained his blood. Which littered the surroundings. His eyes were open, and he had a look of terror frozen on his face. It was clear that he had suffered a terrible death. We were horrified, and we couldn't believe what we were seeing. We were terrified for our lives, knowing that Satoshi did not die a natural death.

We huddled together in shock and fear. We couldn't believe what had just happened and were trying to accept that one of us was gone. The mood was somber and tense as we silently sat until Taro spoke up.

"I think it's the Yuki-Onna," Taro said, his voice low and filled with dread. "I've heard the legends, and all the signs point to her. The snowstorm, the icy breath, the drained blood all fit."

We looked at each other, realizing that Taro was right. The Yuki-Onna was a ghostly spirit associated with winter and snowstorms, known for her icy breath and vampiric tendencies. We had all heard the legends before but never thought they could be true. The thought of being stalked by the Yuki-Onna was terrifying, but we knew we had to face reality and find a way to survive.

"We have to stick together, be alert, and find a way out of here before it's too late," Haruka said, trying to keep us all calm. We knew we were in grave danger, but we had to keep our wits about us to survive. The thought of what had happened to Satoshi was too much to bear.

Act 3: Attempt to Escape

We discussed our alternatives but ultimately decided against repairing our snow vehicle because we knew the Yuki-Onna would return for us. We had to get away quickly.

"I think our best option is to navigate the snowstorm on foot," Taro said, his voice low and filled with determination. "We have a map and compass, and we can use the stars to guide us. We can follow the map and compass to find a safe place."

We all nodded in agreement, knowing that Taro was right. We had no other choice. We knew the snowstorm would be dangerous, but it was better than staying here and waiting for the Yuki-Onna to return for us.

"We have to move fast and stick together," Haruka said, her voice filled with urgency. "We have to find a way out of here before it's too late."

We all knew that time was running out, and we had to act fast to survive. We gathered our things and set out into the snowstorm, our hearts heavy with fear but our determination strong. We knew the Yuki-Onna was out there, and we had to escape her before it was too late.

As we trudged through the snowstorm, we were all on high alert, our hearts pounding with fear. We knew the Yuki-Onna was out there, and we had to be careful. We were making progress, but we were also running out of time.

Suddenly, the Yuki-Onna ambushed us. She appeared out of nowhere, her ghostly figure looming over us.

Haruka and Taro were quick to act. Haruka, being the physically strongest among us, immediately pushed me behind her, shielding me with her body. She brandished a ski pole she had picked up earlier, using it as a makeshift weapon.

Taro, being the most analytical and quick-thinking among us, immediately assessed the situation and used his expertise in outdoor survival. He started a small fire using a fire starter and some branches he had gathered earlier to distract the Yuki-Onna.

The two friends stood shoulder to shoulder, Haruka using her strength to fend off Yuki-Onna's relentless attacks while Taro's flames flickered desperately, trying to keep the icy specter at bay. Their bravery was undeniable, but Yuki-Onna's powers were too formidable. With a sorrowful look, Haruka was struck by a blast of freezing air, her breath turning to mist as she fell. Taro, tears freezing on his cheeks, tried to fight back but was felled by a sharp icicle Yuki-Onna conjured from the snow. In their final moments, they reached out to each other, their hands just inches apart.

Haruka and Taro were both brutally killed in front of me, their screams still ringing in my ears. I was the only one left, and I knew I had to escape, no matter what.

I stumbled and fell, my body wracked with pain. I could feel Yuki-Onna's icy breath on my face. I thought my end was near. But I refused to give up. I pushed myself to my feet and ran, my heart pounding with fear. I didn't look back; I just kept running, and my mind focused on survival. I barely managed to escape, but I was severely injured, both physically and emotionally. The attack was desperate and terrifying, and it was something that would haunt me forever.

Act 4: The Survivor

As I lay in the hospital bed, my mind replayed the events of the past few days over and over again. The memories of Haruka, Taro, and Satoshi's deaths haunted me, and I couldn't shake off the feeling of guilt for being the only survivor. I struggled to come to terms with the trauma and loss I had experienced.

The doctors told me that I was lucky to be alive, but I didn't feel lucky. I felt empty and alone. I knew I had to honor the memories of my friends and make sure that their deaths were not in vain.

I shared my story with the authorities, prompting them to launch a search and rescue operation for my friends. Someone found their bodies and brought them back home for a proper burial. I ensured their families knew the truth about what had happened and how much they meant to me.

As I recovered, I made it my mission to spread awareness about the Yuki-Onna legend and the dangers of the snowy mountains. I wanted to ensure that no one else had to experience the same tragedy that my friends and I had. I also ensured that the resort implemented better safety measures to prevent such an incident from happening again.

I knew that I would never fully heal from the trauma and loss, but I found solace in honoring the memories of Haruka, Taro, and Satoshi. Their deaths will always be a part of me, but I will ensure that their legacies live on and that no one forgets them.

-The End-

When Yuka Nakamura and her friends arrive at the remote Zao Onsen ski resort, they expect a peaceful winter getaway. But as a deadly snowstorm traps them in isolation, they realize they are not alone. A ghostly figure, the Yuki-Onna, haunts the frozen landscape, her icy gaze and chilling presence turning their vacation into a nightmare. One by one, Yuka's friends fall prey to the vengeful spirit, leaving her to face the torment alone. Will Yuka survive the Yuki-Onna's wrath, or will she become just another frozen soul in the snow?

Written by
Jayson R. Valencia
Rodulfo Q. Todio

PRAY... SHE DOESN'T ANSWER.

BLACK MAGIC MARY

JAYSON R. VALENCIA
RODULFO Q. TODIO

Black Magic Mary

In the lush landscapes of Siquijor, known for its mystical traditions and folklore, Mara seeks solace from her tumultuous past and a love potion to win back her estranged husband. Guided by her best friend Clara, a mananambal, she uncovers the dark secrets of a powerful ritual and a statue with a sinister reputation: Black Magic Mary. But as Mara delves deeper into a world of cults and demons, she must confront her deepest fears and the malice threatening to consume her. With revenge on her mind, can Mara escape the grasp of the very darkness she seeks to harness, or will she become a pawn in a deadly game of retribution?

Pray... She doesn't answer.

Prologue

My journey to unimaginable horrors began twenty years ago. It was 1990 when I met my husband, Stan, inside a church where I was offering candles to the Blessed Virgin Mary. I was praying the Holy Rosary as a devotee, and as I was about to finish, when he came near me, lit a candle, and prayed. I smelled his perfume, stared at him, and felt butterflies. I felt giddy and euphoric. He became my first and only boyfriend and then my husband.

We had a lot of fun together, traveling to the beach, watching movies, and spending time inside the church. However, things changed when we married. I discovered he was an alcoholic. He drinks with his pals almost daily at a shop near our house.

I did not see it coming. One day, while in one of his drinking sessions, I came in and tried to ask him to go home because his companions were getting rowdy, and neighbors were already complaining. He got so raging mad at me and punched me in the head in front of everyone. Then he pulled my arm and angrily dragged me home. My lips were busted, and bruises and scrapes covered my body because the concrete road dragged my skin.

In the morning, seeing that I was severely hurt, Stan tended to my sore head, scrapes, and bruises at our house. He promised never to hurt me again, so I forgave him and gave him another chance.

For a while there, things seemed to be getting better. Then we found out that I was pregnant. The news brings joy to Stan. But a few days after that, he returned home intoxicated. He struck me in the stomach after some arguing. With a ruptured uterus, I ended up in the hospital. After the miscarriage, the doctor informed me that I would never be able to have children. I cried like I never cried before; it was the darkest day of my life.

Stan was very apologetic at first and tried to make it up to me by buying me things. Honestly, I don't know what to think at that point.

I can't even comprehend how he could believe that any material things in the world could replace my baby and the damage that doomed me from having any other child again.

His pretenses didn't last, though; later on, I discovered that he was seeing her high school sweetheart. When he left his unlocked phone in the bathroom, I read his text messages and found out he was about to leave me. I cried and asked him not to go, but he told me that I was worthless and he wanted to have children of his own. He left the house that day and never came back. I sobbed as I was alone for several nights, waiting for my husband in the hope he would return, but he didn't.

I was on the verge of committing suicide when a phone call from my best friend, Clara, saved me from taking my own life. It is as if she knows what I'm going through then and urged me to keep going. Clara was my classmate in college, but when we graduated, she returned to her home province. She invited me to a retreat since she knows how much I adore the Blessed Virgin Mary.

She also told me that we could go to mananambals in their province for a love potion so I could let anyone, even my husband, fall in love with me. Rumors suggest that traditional healers in the Philippines, known as Mananambals, can transform into animals for spiritual and medicinal purposes.

I know that no one will ever love me as much as Stan did since I'm overweight and ugly. I embarked on a journey to find a Mananambal who could brew me a love potion in Siquijor. I also wanted to see the famous statue of St. Rita, also known as the Black Magic Mary, which is housed in a nearby church in that area since I believe touching it will bring me miracles.

In my quest for love and healing, I unknowingly stumbled on a terrifying encounter with a demon lurking in the shadows. I discovered a nightmarish world of murderous cults and was the target of their sinister plot. Unspeakable horrors almost consumed my soul. I am Mara; this is my story.

Act 1: The Arrival

It was almost 4 in the afternoon when I arrived at the port of Larena. I saw my best friend Clara sitting on a bench in the arrival waiting area. She was in her usual black dress. She was talking to an old man who resembled her uncle, whom I had seen before when he visited Clara at the university. I waved to them as I walked towards them. Clara smiled and waved back when she noticed me waving.

"Mara! I miss you. It's been a long time," Clara said as she stood up and hurried to hug me. "You remember Uncle Dom?" she pointed to the old man.

"Of course," I replied and smiled at her uncle. Uncle Dom nodded.

Uncle Dom took my belongings and placed them on top of the habal-habal. He mentioned that no other means of transportation existed except tricycles and motorcycles. We rode the tricycle for over an hour on a slick route until we arrived in their village.

I noticed some weird glances from a few people who saw us on the road. Other vehicles and pedestrians gave way when they saw us.

"Am I that ugly?" I asked playfully. "No, it was because of Uncle and me. They respect us here since we are mananambal," Clara answered.

"What is a Mananambal again?" I have to ask because although I have heard the term before, I only have a faint idea.

"Mananambal are traditional healers; the spirits grant us healing powers. It is our calling to use these gifts to cure the sick and bring harmony to our community." Clara explained to me.

"I see," I nodded several times as I answered. I'm religious and believe in miracles, which is not new to me.

When we arrived, I saw Clara built her home with bamboo sticks and an Anahaw leaf roof. I was intrigued by the several colored bottles on their cupboard and wondered what they were.

"That is a herbal medicine my uncle makes," Clara said. "People can't afford hospitalization here, so they go to my uncle for healing.

"You did not tell me that you and your uncle are a Mananambal," I told Clara as I returned the bottle. The term was still running through my mind, so I repeated it.

"I am sure I mentioned it to you when we were in college," Clara mentioned. By the way, are you hungry? There is no fast food restaurant here, but Uncle cooks well."

Uncle Dom placed some barbeque meat, rice, and soup on the table and offered us a meal. Clara then persuaded me to take a seat and eat. The dish was terrific, but it had a strange flavor. "I put some herbs on it to rejuvenate your body," Uncle Dom said, "I know you're tired."

"Do you also make a love potion?" I asked the old man. Uncle Dom and Clara looked at each other and answered simultaneously. "Of course." Clara said, "The locals also go to Uncle for that."

"How much do they pay for it?" I asked curiously. "It is free but has conditions," Uncle Dom answered. Clara interrupted, "I will explain it to you later, and we need to go to the church right away to register for the retreat tonight."

Uncle Dom finished his meal, walked away from the table, and went outside to sharpen his jungle bolo on an improvised chair. A jungle bolo is a type of machete or large knife commonly used for cutting through dense vegetation in tropical jungles in the Philippines. Somehow, Uncle Dom gave me chills now and then as he stared at me.

Act 2: The Devotee

After resting for a while, we went to the Santa Maria Church, which houses the one-of-a-kind Santa Rita de Cascia statue. The image is worth looking at because of its strange aura. The terrible expression on the saint's face, her hand grasping a skull, and the inverted crucifix gave me chills.

"The inverted crucifix symbolizes humility among Christians, " Clara explained. "Even Pope John Paul II used that symbol in his travels in the Middle East." she looked at me as if trying to find out what I was thinking.

"The skull symbolizes death since life is transient," I added to Clara's surprise.

"Oh, you know about this?" Her eyes lit up in amazement at what I just said.

I know these symbolisms, but my first impression of the image was that it was unsettling, strange, and creepy. Santa Rita wore clothes that looked like what the Virgin Mary would wear, but her robe was black and sparkled with shiny gems and sequins. Her cold, empty stare and serious, pale expression instantly scared me. I felt her intense gaze as if she could see right into my soul.

I overheard a tourist from the crowd saying she was a nightwalker, laughing as she said so while trying to scare her companion. She also claims the small religious statue mysteriously vanishes from its glass cabinet. It supposedly occurs at dusk and reappears before dawn.

I decided to take a leap of faith, opened my booklet of devotion to St. Rita, and read the prayers there.

As I was uttering a prayer of reconciliation, I saw a group of people in black dress venerating Santa Rita outside the chapel. I also noticed mud in the icon's dress and feet. I cleaned them with my handkerchief, hoping she would grant my wish.

As I stood in line, anxiously waiting to register for the retreat, I leaned in and asked the woman in charge if the people ahead of us were also mananambals. She whispered that they were Mambabarangs in hushed tones. Gripping my hand tightly, Clara hurriedly pulled me away, insisting that she had already registered me. Her sudden irritation and warning that I didn't speak to anyone else bewildered me.

On our way to Clara's house, I mentioned to her that I felt a strong connection with St. Rita because we both had experiences with abusive husbands. Curious, Clara asked me, "Did you know that bees surrounded her when she was just a baby?" she paused and continued, "The bees went in and out of her mouth without hurting her," she added.

She saw my curious reaction to her last statement, "That's not all; rumors say that the skull he's carrying belongs to her husband." she looked directly into my eyes for a few seconds.

I was so creeped out with that information that I broke eye contact and tried to change the subject of the conversation.

"I learned that her real name is Margarita, which means pearl," I smiled to ease the atmosphere.

Clara quickly responded, "Do you know the meaning of your name, Mara?" I heard tension in her voice; it was clear that she was trying to provoke me. I was so confused. At the same time, I fell silent because I knew that my name connotes two things: anguish over the loss of a husband and defiance of God.

We both met the rest of the travel with an awkward silence.

Act 3: The Revelation

After a few minutes, we arrived at Clara's house. As I stepped in, an unsettling feeling washed over me. The air was heavy with the scent of incense, swirling around the room in a thick haze. Uncle Dom stood before the altar, engaged in a mysterious ritual. At the altar, I saw a miniature replica of Santa Rita's icon adorned with delicate Sampaguita flowers and food offerings.

While Uncle Dom immersed himself in prayer, a swarm of bees emerged from nowhere, drawing closer to him. My heart pounded as I watched in terror as the bees boldly entered and emerged from his mouth, leaving him unharmed. The sight sent shivers down my spine, leaving me deeply unsettled.

Uncle Dom abruptly concluded his prayer, his gaze fixating on Clara and me as we entered the room. The intensity of the moment hung in the air.

"You are my best friend, Mara, and I hope I can trust you," Clara said as she grabbed my left arm, her voice filled with emotion. She glanced at her uncle, who gave her a savage look. She nodded and continued, "Yes, we are mananambals, but we belonged to a higher level."

"We are Mambabarangs. Our skill set is way higher than that of the Mananambals. We believe in the universal values of justice, freedom, and equality. We help suffering people like you," Clara revealed.

"You should punish your husband for his wrongdoings," Uncle Dom remarked as he stood up and walked away from the altar. "He does not deserve your love."

For a moment, I felt numb. Memories of my spouse's violent actions, like being smacked across the face and punched in the stomach, rushed back to me. The pain felt so real, as if it was happening all over again, and I couldn't hold back my tears.

"Our patron saint, Santa Rita, will help you." Clara urged me. "But you have to be brave and let him go. It's tough to leave an abusive spouse. It often seems like you're failing, or that you're hurting your family, or that you're not trying hard enough, or that you're not giving your spouse a second opportunity."

"We can be your own family, Mara." Uncle Dom said in a convincing tone. "Allow us to avenge your sufferings."

I was in a mix of conflicting emotions. On one hand, I feel a glimmer of hope and relief that someone is offering assistance and understanding of my pain. On the other hand, I also have hesitation and doubt, knowing how difficult it is to leave an abusive spouse. However, avenging my sufferings stirred up a deep well of anger in me, tempting me with thoughts of retribution. I saw two memories collide in my mind: one of my husband laughing and singing with his friends, carefree and content, while the other showed me trapped in the suffocating loneliness of our home, enduring pain and despair. As I tended to my wounds, a haunting image consumed me—my husband sharing an intimate connection with another woman. The moment his fist struck me, a surge of agony surged through me, and I was consumed by wrath so fierce it bordered on murderous rage.

"If you open this bottle, you're agreeing to seek justice for what you've been through. We'll make sure those who deserve it face the consequences. These insects will summon others to enter your ex-husband's body. They'll eat away at his flesh while he's still alive, causing a slow death," Uncle Dom explained, handing me a bottle filled with insects.

I held onto the bottle tightly, wiping my tears away. With a firm resolve, I opened it and said a prayer to Santa Rita, the patron saint of Mambabarangs, seeking justice for what my husband had done. But as soon as I opened the bottle, the insects flew and crawled onto my arms, causing me to drop them on the floor. I quickly apologized to Clara and

Uncle Dom; feeling exhausted and needing rest, I went to my room. The next thing I knew, I had blacked out on my bed.

Act 4: The Retreat

The next day, we went to the retreat location, a short distance from the church. At first glance, a completely different set of people organized this meeting than those I saw in the church earlier in the morning. There were none of those familiar, friendly, and welcoming faces that I interacted with. On the contrary, the staff on this retreat had a cold and somewhat fierce look on their faces.

Unlike the usual structures in this countryside, which use wood or bamboo as materials, builders constructed this chapel from limestone.

Clara accompanied me in one empty chair beside a few other tourists who registered for this religious activity. "Sit here, I'll be outside." she blurted out and immediately left.

I glanced at Clara's Uncle, whispering to some male staff wearing their jungle bolo.

Black candles lit before the altar, casting a crimson glow on its surroundings.

A few other tourists mentioned that they wanted to go to the church to view the statue of Santa Rita after the lecture; however, a staff member who heard this rebuked them and told them that we should not go near the statue at night.

Being tourists that we are, this reprimand stokes our curiosity even more.

The lectures were boring and uneventful, so everyone was relieved that the proctor declared a fifteen-minute break so that we could go to the washroom and grab some food.

Once outside, I, along with a few other guests, sneaked into the church to inspect the statue of Santa Rita. We hesitated because the church was locked and well-secured, and we could hear some movement inside. Nonetheless, our curiosity got the best of us, and we broke one of the windows to get in.

It was pitch black inside. We used the light from a black candle that one of the tourists had taken from the altar to find our way to the altar where the statue stood. But when we got there, the statue was not in its place. Someone suggested they store it in a room inside the church, so we decided to find it.

When we hear something, we are all scattered inside the church, looking for doors.

On the far left corner of the altar, we noticed, behind the shadows, a veiled figure intently watching us. I swear I could see it grinning at us from that dark area. We all stopped and stared in panic. After all, breaking in is a criminal offense. The figure slowly stepped forward, making an eerie sound of wood breaking at every step. There's something wrong with the way it moved. It seems forced, jagged, and angular, with every step revealing the dark yellow laces on top of its black dress. We all gasped. It was the statue of Santa Rita of Casia.

What comes next is something straight out of horror movies.

Then, suddenly, out of nowhere, it lunged forward with an unimaginable speed and ferocity towards our nearest male companion. The statue grabbed his neck and immediately started shoving the crucifix in its left hand on the throat of the guy. It kept on stabbing his throat, the next one more forceful than the previous. After that, it lifted him like a rag doll and single-handedly severed his neck away from his body.

People could hear our cries from miles away. Everyone scrambled outside the window where we had come from, screaming for help.

Once outside, in shock and disbelief, I noticed that the surrounding houses near the church were closing their doors and windows as well as their lights. Behind the trees, darkly dressed figures appeared, like those women in the church earlier. One of them lit a torch and started shouting at us while pointing her fingers in our direction. Like the statue, her movement was also peculiarly forced, jagged, and angular.

There was now a chorus of shouts coming from the residents. Then it hit me: they were not just shouting. They are hexing us with curses. Some of the mambabarangs opened jars filled with every unimaginable creepy critter.

The insects swarmed the terrified tourists, invading their bodies through every opening they could find. They pierced their noses, ears, mouths, and skin, feasting on them from the inside. We were forced into the stone chapel as the organizers and staff gathered the survivors. Strangely, not a single insect came near me.

I was shaking so much; tears were pouring down my face out of sheer fear. I saw Clara inside, "What's happening, Clara?" I sobbed as I spoke. Clara just stood there looking at me. At the back, I saw Uncle Dom and some of the staff he talked to earlier. I gasped when I saw them hack the remaining tourists to death.

Terror filled me, and tears streamed down my face as I realized that I was the only one remaining alive. Then Clara stepped forward and stopped within a few paces away from me. She slowly raised her right hand, holding something familiar. "Mara, look, your curse worked!" she smiled menacingly and continued. "Don't you recognize this? It is the head of your husband." she shrieks in unintelligible language after that. I half fainted when I realized what I was looking at. Only to be jolted back to consciousness by a punch in the face coming from Uncle Dom.

"We haven't finished with you, Mara. We will carve from your body the next image of our patron, Santa Rita of Casia." Uncle Dom said while wiping the blood of the murdered tourists from his jungle bolo.

"That's why you're here, Mara! You are a perfect example of our Santa Rita; the abuse you suffered from your husband proves it." Clara whispered this to me in a calm voice.

I screamed at the top of my lungs, desperately hoping that someone would come to our aid, praying that someone would hear our cries and call the police. My voice echoed through the empty streets, filled with fear and desperation.

"No one would help you, Mara. The locals are terrified of our powers," said Uncle Dom as he stooped down to drag the body of one of the dead tourists outside the chapel.

They locked me up in the stone chapel. I was praying the Holy Rosary and asking for the intercession of the Blessed Virgin Mary when I noticed an opening in the corner of the chapel. At the same time, I heard a commotion outside. It gave me enough space and cover to squeeze out and escape. I kept running and did not look back.

Epilogue

After the incident, I heard about a police investigation on the news, but it led nowhere. Fear consumed me, and I hid, unsure if I could even trust the local police. I solemnly promised myself I would never return to that dreadful place again. However, one day, an article caught my eye while reading the newspaper. It featured the "Saint Rita of Cascia in Siquijor," as I gazed at the image, a faint smile crept onto my face. The resemblance between the Black Magic Mary of Siquijor and my dear friend Clara was striking.

-The End-

In the eerie depths of Siquijor, Mara's quest for truth leads her into the sinister world of black magic and ancient curses. When a mysterious cult and a vengeful demon entwine her fate, survival becomes a deadly game. Worshiping a Demon: The Black Magic Mary of Siquijor delves into the heart of Filipino folklore, where betrayal, fear, and the supernatural collide. Will Mara escape the darkness, or will she become its next victim?

Written by
Jayson R. Valencia
Rodulfo Q. Todio

MISSING
BACKPACKERS
JAYSON R. VALENCIA
RODULFO Q. TODIO

Missing Backpackers

When two backpackers, eager to experience the myths and mysteries of Southeast Asia, arrive in a remote village in the Philippines, they find themselves drawn to local legends of the Aswang—a bloodthirsty creature from folklore. But what begins as an exciting adventure soon spirals into a waking nightmare. As one vanishes and the other stumbles upon a horrifying secret deep within the village, survival becomes a desperate game of life and death. In this chilling tale of fear, myth, and the unknown, you'll learn why some people should never explore certain places.

People should never follow some legends... especially when they're hungry.

Introduction

I love backpacking because it allows me to socialize like nothing else at home. Unlike backpacking, where you could meet different people and cultures, you are usually only limited to close-knit people within your circle at home.

One of the people I met during my backpacking adventures was Joshua. We met each other in Thailand and have been backpacking together since. I was one of those thrifty backpackers who had to budget my resources because I didn't have a regular income in Maine. Of course, my lifestyle played a big part; getting a day job when traveling is tough.

Joshua taught me everything I know about being a thrifty backpacker; for example, he introduced me to staying in cheap hostels or dorms instead of the more pricey hotels.

Joshua was a fellow American who grew up in Alabama. He was a guy who always carried a guitar with him anywhere we went. If anyone asked him to play it, he would laugh. He told me that he had it only to charm girls. He didn't know how to play it; heck, he didn't even know how to tune it. He always told me we needed to fake it until we made it. He told me how he considered his guitar his most prized possession because it was a limited edition Rainsong BI-WS1000N1 Black Ice Series. It was super expensive, but he got it cheap from one of his backpacker friends. In his own words, "I would be dead before anyone could take this away from me," he jokingly said while stroking the neck of his guitar. We both laughed.

Anyway, this was our sixth time visiting Southeast Asia. We would see the more well-known locations in Thailand, Vietnam, and Bali in Indonesia. But this time, we both agreed that it was time to experience a different culture and experience.

We were also intrigued by the rumors about the demonic creatures called "Aswang" at our destination. Although we didn't believe in the supernatural, experiencing a culture where the myth of mystical creatures like the Aswangs is the main tourist attraction enamored us. An aswang is a terrifying creature from Philippine folklore. It is said to be a shape-shifter that can take on various forms, often resembling a monstrous creature or a hideous humanoid. It preys on human meat and is said to be able to take on a human form.

It was the morning of June 6 when we arrived at Roxas Airport in Capiz City, Philippines; there were no direct flights to our destination, so we had to travel to Manila first and then fly to Roxas from there. Despite being tired, we had high hopes and were excited about our next adventure. Nothing prepared us for the horror we soon encountered in Capiz, Philippines.

Act 1: The Inn

When we reached Capiz City, we checked in at the Betina Manor Inn. Although it was one of the cheapest in the area, it exceeded our budget.

Our strategy was to settle in, get acquainted with our fellow tourists who knew the area better, and get their advice. Then, we would transfer to the cheaper alternative as soon as possible.

Betina Manor was a shitty place, indeed. The online reviews were as accurate as they can get. Firstly, the area was in the red light district. So there were hookers everywhere. I understand this place would have been fine for some tourists looking for a short stay. But this was a deal-breaker for us, who genuinely wanted to experience the culture and be there longer. As for the establishment itself, the bed was small, the sheets had stains, there was no shower, and there was no flush for the toilet. That in itself was a horror story.

For all its faults, Betina Manor certainly made up for its excellent customer service. Most of the staff were very friendly and ensured that your stay was enjoyable—all except for one guy, Romy!

Romy was one of the attendants; he was one of those people with whom you would immediately sense that there was something odd in how he interacted. There was always a sly grin on his face. You could feel that he calculated his movements. Whenever he looked at you, there seemed to be a glint of deceit. In hindsight, I would say that this is why he never looked anyone directly in the eyes. I noticed that even his workmates used to avoid him. Nonetheless, according to the other tourists, Romy was the man to talk to if you wanted cheaper accommodation somewhere away from the red-light district. With this in mind, I knew we would have to deal with him sooner or later.

Over the next few days, most other tourists we saw talking to Romy had already checked out of Betina Manor. One day, while having breakfast, Joshua told me he had spoken to Romy the night before. The attendant offered a small hut in a village near the mangrove forest. The only catch was that, at the time, only one bed was vacant. Joshua asked me if it was okay if he went there first because his funds were almost gone. He desperately needed to get a cheaper place to stay.

I understood where Joshua was coming from because I was almost out of funds as well. I told Joshua it was okay and I'd follow him there later if there were another vacancy. He tapped me on the back and thanked me.

That afternoon, Joshua picked up his guitar and said his farewell. "See you there," I assured him. He smiled, slipped a piece of paper into my pocket, and replied, "See you soon, bro."

Act 2: The Address

A week later, I finally decided that it was time to approach Romy and ask him if I had any available accommodation. At first, he tried to ignore me, but when I repeated the question, he stopped what he was doing and looked at me from head to toe. He didn't answer my question and returned to what he was doing. I thought that, being a native, he might not understand what I was saying. So I tapped him on the shoulder and asked him again.

"I'm friends with Joshua, one of the guys who went with you a few days earlier." I slightly raised my voice and ensured I was pronouncing things correctly.

Romy suddenly stopped what he was doing and faced me. By the look on his face, I got that he was pissed. "Fuck off, man!" He yelled out. His reaction shocked me because I was sure I did nothing for him to react to me like that. To say that I was surprised by his sudden hostility towards me is an understatement. I looked around and saw other tourists looking at us with bewildered faces.

To avoid humiliating myself further, I decided to back off and go to my room. When I arrived inside, I sat on the bed to think of what I did to be at the receiving end of Romy's wrath. I shook my head because I couldn't think of anything that I did wrong.

That's when I remembered the paper Joshua slipped into my pocket while leaving. I carefully took it out and saw an address written on it.

"Alright," I said to myself. I'll bypass the middleman, then. I decided to go straight to the address and ask for accommodation.

Act 3: The Village

That afternoon, I decided to pack my things up and check out of the hostel. Apart from the hotel not meeting my expectations, the unresolved dispute with Romy was the final nail in the coffin.

I hopped on a motorcycle taxi and asked the driver to take me to the next village, as shown on the small piece of paper that Joshua had given me. The driver read the paper, looked at me, and warned me to be careful. After 30 minutes of riding, I found myself in a remote village a few meters away from the forest. Lush greenery surrounded the town, which offered a serene and peaceful escape from bustling city life. Houses were traditional, and builders mostly made them from bamboo grass. I was elated, especially since it was so near to the forest. Trekking through it later ran through my mind.

I asked the driver how much I owed him for the fare. He ignored my question and nervously stared at the old, weathered sign with faded letters in front of the village.

"Sir, don't go in there; I'll bring you back," his voice cracked.

"I have a friend here," I warily explained because I thought he was trying to scam me.

He looked at me and stared at the sign again.

"Is that the name of the village?" I asked, trying to clear the tension in the air.

"Yes, sir," he whispered. He cleared his throat. "I'm going back, sir. Please be careful." Then, he immediately jumped on his motorcycle and made a U-turn.

"Wait, I haven't paid you yet." I raised my hand to call him. I knew he heard me because he was just a few meters away but didn't look back.

I scratched my head, wondering what that was all about. I saw a few people doing daily chores as I entered the village. Some were tending to their fields or livestock. As I walked deeper into the town, everyone stopped what they were doing and stared at me. I tried talking to a few locals, but they met me with cold looks and sharp replies. The people in this village were not friendly at all, unlike other places I had been to in this country. I told myself that since the town was remote, the people there were not accustomed to seeing foreigners like me. But I remembered many tourists who had transferred accommodation in this area, so that could not have been the case. I kept walking as I ignored the stares that I got from the locals.

As I scanned the surroundings, I noticed three middle-aged women dressed in black dresses. They were running in my direction and had black scarves on their heads. They stopped a few meters away from me and started shouting at me while raising their hands and pointing their fingers at me. I could see hate in their eyes, more like what I saw when Romy looked at me. "Are they cursing me?" I asked myself.

The heat increased as the sun beat down relentlessly, causing me to feel dizzy. My brain whirled, partly from the sweltering heat and partly from the overwhelming worry of the scenario I had unintentionally landed in. A sense of foreboding compelled me to act quickly, and I made the rash decision to turn left, my pulse thumping within my chest.

My footsteps echoed ominously in the quiet streets as I accelerated my pace. The once tranquil village suddenly felt forlorn. The surrounding trees' shadows stretched and twisted, twisting the familiar picture into something strange. The air became dense with an unidentified stench, a cross between rotting and something more horrible.

As I continued, a sight struck horror deep within me and assaulted my senses. What was before me looked like a horrible mound of discarded rubbish, a macabre assemblage of discarded fragments? As I bore witness to the horrors that lay within the pile, my stomach churned, and bile erupted in my throat.

I gasped in fear among the debris. A once-pristine Rainsong BI-WS1000N1 Black Ice Series guitar lay there, smeared with crimson and shattered. The strings, which had once been musical instruments, now hung limply like harbingers of doom. A shiver ran down my spine when I saw this wasn't an accident or an act of vandalism. Something far more horrible had occurred in this desolate location.

My gaze drifted to the torn and smoldering backpacks strewn haphazardly nearby. They were the remains of other travelers, backpackers like me, who had met a tragic end. The splatterings of what seemed to be blood that graced the surrounding region mingled with the remains of their belongings. The spectacle in front of me was a terrifying display of violence and sorrow.

A surge of paralyzing fear engulfed me, rendering me motionless and helpless. Panic clawed at my throat as I desperately tried to comprehend the unspeakable horror that had unfolded in this forsaken corner of the world. But before I could gather my wits, a chilling sound pierced the air—heavy and hurried footsteps closing in on my location.

Every instinct within me screamed to flee, to escape the clutches of the impending threat. With my heart racing and my breath catching in shallow gasps, I turned on my heels, desperately seeking refuge from the encroaching darkness that threatened to consume me.

I dashed to the nearest pathway and strolled, pretending not to see those bloodied items.

"What are you doing here?" a bald old man, probably in his 70s, asked me. A few middle-aged men accompanied him, staring at me intently.

I looked around me to make sure that they were talking to me. When I was sure they were questioning me, I answered, "I'm hoping to find cheap accommodation." I bit my lips and thought about asking the old man about Joshua, but I decided against it.

The old man looked at one of his friends and said, "I can help you with that." He turned to face me and asked, "Tell me, are you looking for someone, perhaps your friend who came into this village?

"No, I'm alone. I don't know anyone. I just tried to find cheaper accommodation away from the city." I lied.

"Okay then, 200 pesos per day; these three will accompany you to your hut," the old man motioned to his companion.

The way they stared at me made me question whether I should accept the offer or return to the city. However, it felt like this wasn't an offer that I could accept or decline. I couldn't think because I was so stressed. I felt that they were leading me to my death.

I followed them to the hut, trying to act as casually as possible.

Act 4: The Feast

I did not leave the hut the whole day; I did not eat because there was nothing to eat there. I was too afraid to go out. Luckily, there was a jug of water, which I devoured. I was determined to wait until nighttime and then run for it.

Throughout the day, I heard men moving around my hut. They circled the area, maintaining constant vigilance without uttering a single word. They only left around 7 p.m., probably to eat. I could hear that there was a celebration happening in the village. The sound of voices singing and drums beating filled the air. The rhythmic pounding of drums grew louder and faster, creating an unsettling pulse that seemed to echo in my ears. They were more like demonic chants.

"Now's my chance," I whispered, heart pounding. With the ceremony outside facing my door, I knew I couldn't risk using it. The hut, made of dried grass, was a good thing. I used to carry a small Swiss army knife that I usually used as a screwdriver. It looked like I could use it to poke a hole in the wall. I took it from my bag's pocket and carefully started cutting a hole in the wall. It took a while, but I managed to do it. I hurriedly threw my backpack outside, hoping no one would notice. I paused to ensure no one had heard the bag hitting the ground. Then, I squeezed my body through the opening.

I hid behind the hut's wall and waited a minute to ensure no one was looking in my direction. After that, breathless and shaking, I quickly hid at the forest's edge. My heart raced as I tried to calm down and figure out what to do next. I was relieved that no one noticed me darting to the shrubs. But curiosity got the better of me, and I cautiously peeked at the celebration.

At first, I couldn't figure out what I was seeing; I only noticed the dimly lit torches cast flickering shadows on the crowd. A horrifying sight slowly appeared as my eyes adjusted to the scene. The villagers' faces twisted as if they were no longer human. Dark hair covered their bodies, and their nails looked like sharp claws. While I was trying to make sense of what I saw, all of a sudden, the drumming stopped.

One of the villagers dragged a guy in the middle; I knew the guy!! He was a tourist, a French national. I saw him talking to Romy at the hostel a few days back. I saw the guy crying profusely. He fell to his knees and clasped his hands together pleadingly. His voice trembled in desperation, although I couldn't hear what he said. However, I could see the terror on his face. I froze in fear of what was going to happen next. I saw the old man who had talked to me earlier. He sneaked behind the tourist and drew his machete from a wooden scabbard tied behind his waist. I gasped as I saw him raise his blade and swiftly drop it on the man's neck. The tourist's head rolled on the ground. There was loud cheering and shouting as his body fell to the ground. I could see the bloodlust in everyone's eyes. What happened next scarred me for life. One by one, the locals started carving meat from his body and proceeded to eat it with fresh blood oozing from their lips. They reveled in their gruesome feast as they devoured the flesh; unsettling chants and disturbing music once again filled the air. I could feel the terror gripping my heart as I slowly started to realize the true nature of these people.

The celebration was completely fixated on me that I failed to notice a man and three women dressed in black approaching my hut, whom I had seen earlier.

I wanted to run, but I was too afraid that any movement on my part would immediately alert them of my presence in the shrubs. I was trembling uncontrollably; my breath came in short gasps.

All of a sudden, they halted right under the dimly lit torch in front of the hut. And the guy started stripping naked. One of the old women passed a vessel that looked like a buffalo horn. He poured what seemed like an oily liquid on his palms. As he started applying the liquid to his body, the light from the torch illuminated his face, leaving me aback and in utter shock! It was Romy, the same guy who worked at the hotel.

The realization hit me like a bolt of lightning, and suddenly, the puzzle pieces started fitting together in my mind. Was Romy's role in the hotel nothing but a facade? Was he luring unsuspecting backpackers here, only to subject them to a horrifying fate?

The three old women abruptly diverted my attention by beginning to chant. Their eerie voices filled the air as they raised their hands towards Romy.

I watched in complete terror as Romy started changing right before my eyes. His body twisted and distorted, becoming something monstrous. His skin turned pale and grey, veins appearing all over. His eyes became empty and glowed.

With a horrifying scream, His mouth stretched open, revealing sharp and jagged teeth. All the knowledge I had gathered about the Aswang flooded my mind then. I vividly remember reading about them, even laughing at the thought that it was merely the product of someone's wild imagination. And yet, I was face to face with the unimaginable horrors I once dismissed as mere fiction.

Fear paralyzed me. Every fiber of my being urged me to flee, yet I found myself unable to tear my gaze away from the horrifying scene unfolding before me.

The old woman gestured, directing Romy's attention towards my hut. Dread filled me as the three grotesque creatures began advancing, their steps slow and deliberate. With each movement, my anxiety heightened. I felt a cold sweat trickle down my forehead as I saw the remaining men surrounding the entrance of my hut. They drew their machetes, and their eyes fixated on the door, ready to unleash unimaginable horror on me.

I was so afraid that I dropped my backpack and made a run for it toward the jungle. I ran to the north until dawn. I did not stop for anything; luckily, poisonous snakes did not bite me. I ended up in the nearest province, Aklan. I felt disoriented and out of place. I tried to avoid people as much as possible because I was too traumatized.

After an eternity of aimlessly walking the streets, I stared at a makeshift police station. I went inside and asked for help. From there, I called the embassy and tried to narrate everything to the staff on the other end of the call. I may have jumbled my thoughts in panic because she asked me to calm down and repeat what I was trying to say. I tried it again, and my nerves calmed slightly this time. Once she heard it, I could tell she was trying to hide her laughter. "My God, she's not taking my report seriously," I shook my head as I whispered to myself. The staff noticed I paused, so she cleared her throat and answered professionally. She said it's tough to keep track of backpackers because they jump from location to location. They assured me that Joshua would turn up soon in the neighboring provinces. I shook my head because deep inside, I knew that something terrible happened to him.

I returned to the USA feeling shattered. The events of that night kept haunting my mind. I can't believe what I saw that night. To this day, I still question whether what I saw that night was real or not. There's one thing I'm sure of, though: I'm lucky to be alive today. However, it aches in my heart to know that I will never find my friend Joshua.

In June 2004, two American backpackers, Damon and Joshua, embark on an adventure to explore the remote villages of Capiz, Philippines, lured by the eerie legends of the Aswang, a mythical creature said to haunt the region. But what begins as an exciting cultural exploration quickly turns into a nightmare when Joshua mysteriously disappears, leaving Damon alone to face a terrifying reality. As Damon delves deeper into the village's dark secrets, he encounters a horrifying ritual that blurs the line between myth and reality. Trapped and surrounded by menacing villagers with malevolent intent, Damon must fight to escape a fate too horrifying to imagine. Missing Backpackers is a gripping tale of fear, survival, and the sinister power of folklore.

Written by
Jayson R. Valencia
Rodulfo Q. Todio

JAYSON R. VALENCIA
RODULFO Q. TODIO

TYANAK'S
TERROR

AN INNOCENT CRY IN THE
NIGHT HIDES THE TEETH
OF A MONSTER.

Tiyanak's Terror

In a quiet, seemingly peaceful neighborhood, a horrific discovery shatters the calm when a baby is found alone, covered in blood, leading to the gruesome remains of its parents. But as the police attempt to make sense of the tragedy, a more profound, darker secret begins to unfold. What starts as an act of kindness quickly becomes a nightmare when the child's true nature reveals itself.—a creature born from Filipino folklore with an insatiable hunger for flesh. As terror takes hold, no one is safe from the ancient evil that has awakened. An innocent cry in the night hides the teeth of a monster.

Prologue

As the group approaches the source of the crying, their pace slows down, and their eyes lock on the tiny, helpless infant lying amongst the bushes. One of them, a young woman with tears, can't bear the thought of leaving the baby alone.

"Oh my God, what happened to this poor baby?" she asks, her voice trembling with emotion.

Another friend, a young man with a somber expression, kneels beside the infant and carefully examines its body.

"It looks like someone has abandoned it here for a while," he says, his voice filled with sadness. "We have to do something to help it."

As they approach closer, the crying suddenly stops, and the baby's face twists into an eerie, unsettling expression. The group exchanges fearful glances, unsure of what to do next.

"What's wrong with its face?" one of them asks, her voice quivering with fear.

"I don't know," the young man replies, his voice barely above a whisper. "But we have to be careful. Something doesn't feel right about this."

Despite the unease in the air, the young woman steps forward and extends her arms to the infant.

"Come here, little one," she coos softly. "We won't hurt you."

As she reaches out to pick up the infant, its face contorts again, this time into a twisted, evil grin. The group jumps back in fear, their hearts pounding in their chests.

"What is happening?" the young woman cries out, her voice shaking with terror.

As the friends stumble backward, they see the baby's body twist and contort unnaturally, its skin turning a sickly shade of green. The creature's eyes blaze with an otherworldly fire, revealing rows of razor-sharp teeth, baring them in a vicious snarl.

The tiyanak's limbs elongate and contort, growing taller and more menacing by the second. Its once-innocent cries are replaced by deafening shrieks that pierce the stillness of the forest, causing birds to take flight and animals to flee in terror.

The friends freeze in terror, unable to comprehend the horror before them. They feel the hot breath of the tiyanak on their skin as it lunges toward them, its clawed hands reaching out to tear them apart.

The forest echoes with bones cracking and flesh tearing as the tiyanak unleashes fury upon the hapless friends. They scream in agony as they feel its sharp claws slicing through their skin and tearing at their flesh. The sickening scent of blood and death fills the air.

Act 1: The Birth of Chaos

Towering stars shine brightly throughout the low-lying sky. The only sounds on Earth are rustling foliage and nocturnal animal movements. Other than that, it is as quiet as the dead of night until a scream comes from a bungalow.

AIIIEEEE!

Lita is uncontrollably crying as she is about to give birth. The village midwife is asking her to breathe out to expel the baby from her womb. Her husband Melencio is just outside the door with his arm clasped, anxious about what is happening inside the room.

"No way." Melencio couldn't believe it; the baby wasn't due for another two months.

Lita held onto her stomach. "The water already broke," she sounded hysterical while she continued to bleed heavily. Each contraction felt like a bowling ball landing full force on her spine, rolling down her spine while maintaining the initial force, and then landing in her pelvic area with twice the initial force.

"Let's go!" the midwife tried to calm her down.

"I think she's coming, curse you, Melencio, ahhhhh!" Lita calls her husband as she barely could stand the pain. The cramps become more intense and get progressively more challenging and more substantial until it feels like someone is ripping her insides out from the inside. It feels like a hot butter knife is scraping away at her insides, and a million dull needles are puncturing her lower back.

Lita recalls every detail of her relationship with Melencio to numb the pain. Her spouse compelled her to marry him rather than ever courting her. She remembers her wedding day as being among her most depressing moments.

Act 2: The Portent of Doom

The couple had a disastrous wedding. The wedding was in June. They expected a hot, sunny day, but it was a significant storm. Lita is not happy during her wedding ceremony. Her newlywed sister was surprised when they learned she was pregnant and did not attend it. Filipino superstition says it will bring bad luck, as Lita's sister and her wedding happened in the same year. But since she got pregnant, Melencio has to marry her to avoid social disgust. Her parents arranged the marriage because they were a traditional family.

Although Lita doesn't believe in superstitions, she foresees an unhappy marriage. Melencio, a known thug in the area, forced Lita one night to come with him and made her his wife. The townspeople fear Melencio, so no one dares to challenge him. Lita agreed to marry him out of fear or embarrassment.

People rumored that Lita would live a miserable married life because she wore pearls on her wedding day. She didn't smile during the ceremony but remained stunningly beautiful in her long white dress and jet-black hair.

During the wedding reception, Lita also ignored the superstition that she should have a first bite at the cake since she has lactose intolerance or an allergy to sugar. People say that a bride shouldn't skip the first piece of the wedding cake if she wants to avoid difficulties getting pregnant. The bride must take the first bite of the cake as they cut it because it represents fertility.

The wedding colors were red and black. The white wedding cake's red frosting leaked, giving the impression that the dessert was bleeding. While eating the cake, the visitors appeared to be gorging on flesh.

When the couple proceeded to unbox their gifts, they were delighted to see different household items, but the visitors whispered to each other when they opened a gift with a knife set. Gifts like knives and other pointed things are said to bring bad luck in the Philippines. The wedding ceremony, from the prelude to the reception, was a portent of doom.

Act 3: A Dangerous Pregnancy

Melencio called his wife's name and searched every part of the house, including the bedroom, living room, dining room, and kitchen, but when he returned home, he could not find her.

He went to their backyard, where he spotted her collecting all the sun-dried garments. She was wearing a duster and was seven months pregnant. He sighs as he moves towards her and takes all the items.

She was a little surprised to see her spouse there.

"Why do you always arrive like this? I'm easily frightened?"Lita frowned.

"I'm sorry, but how often have I advised you not to wash clothes? You're in your first trimester of pregnancy and tend to become weary easily. Why don't you ever listen to me?" Melencio complained.

"Please don't reprimand me; you do most of the housework when you get home. I feel bad and want to assist you," Lita answered.

In response to his wife's insistence, he sighs and shakes his head. He loves Lita, and at the back of his mind, he appreciates that she is now willing to help him despite her difficult pregnancy.

Lita's pregnancy was challenging for her because she couldn't accept or comprehend it. She didn't anticipate becoming a mother at 22, just as her career was about to take off. Her pregnancy was a rollercoaster of emotions. She always feels unpleasant. Her feet swell. Her boobs expand. Her belly enlarges. She couldn't settle down to sleep. She can't breathe well when the baby grows because it presses against her diaphragm. After she got married, she missed social gatherings and would sit and sob uncontrollably. She couldn't go anywhere, so her life stopped, and she hated it. She was always a very independent woman who took charge of things.

She wasn't able to eat any kind of meat; even the smell made her throw up. So, apart from daily nausea, it got worse when her husband was eating something she didn't like near her.

She also had a tiny belly. The news that the baby would have an issue made her feel like she wasn't getting the whole pregnancy experience. It caused her to experience various moments of stress about her baby's health.

Lita felt contempt toward her husband. This intense hatred or abhorrence is distinct from being irritated. Regardless of the situation, it frequently entails ignoring or discrediting practically all of what her husband has to say while huffing and rolling her eyes during conversation. Having her husband around makes her feel as though she is crawling out of her skin at worst, and it is evident that she does not find anything admirable about him.

Lita was shocked when she found out the blood results of her nuchal scan for her unborn baby. The doctor was shaking her head, saying the blood results had come back showing a high risk of a genetic disorder. She felt the sudden terror that coursed through her spine and the confusion about what the genetic disorder even was. The doctor confided to them that the unborn child could have significant physical and intellectual problems. She also emphasized that, if they make it out of the womb at all, many babies with the genetic disorder pass away in the first few days or weeks of life. The baby then is not compatible with life.

Lita was willing to sacrifice her life for her child. Her mother's heart reigned supreme amidst this trial. But His husband Melencio closed his fist in anger upon hearing the result while his head bowed down. He did not take the challenge properly. He left his wife in the hospital and decided to walk alone by himself.

Act 4: Aborted Abortion

Melencio twisted and knotted his hands as he peered at them from below as if doing so would calm the turmoil he was experiencing. He and others trying to stifle their agony by biting down on their worries caused despair to permeate the space. There is a lot of shouting, ruptures that reach the anal sphincters, more screaming, cursing, sweat, blood, mucus, and general gore. Everything on Lita's insides, even the intestines, is pushed out of the way.

Lita woke him up and told him that he was having a nightmare. He looked at his wife and saw her protruding belly. He remembers the result of the pre-natal test. They are bound to have a child with a genetic disorder. He was also worried about the dangers of keeping the child.

"I don't want to lose you," Melencio murmured. "I'd rather have you than that child."

Lita was silent at first but later replied. "I don't want to abort the baby."

But Melencio has already decided to abort the pregnancy. In the Philippines, it is illegal to have an abortion, so Melencio turned to the street drugs he bought close to a church. It consists of a pill and herbal drink that Lita must take twice daily. Unbeknownst to Melencio, Lita did not take the medications. She decided to continue her pregnancy. She always feels nauseous as her belly grows.

During one of their planned appointments, they went to the ob-gyn, where the medical professional prepared Lita's belly for some imaging. After some time, he said that his ultrasound equipment was giving him some problems, making it difficult to record the heartbeat. Lita questioned whether everything was okay when he started his ultrasound screening and what felt like a lifetime later. Melencio then inquired, "So is the baby okay..." to which he said, "No, the baby is dead. Yet, there is something extremely intriguing going on here that I am attempting to understand. There is some movement."

Because the heartbeat was intermittent, the doctor was unable to provide the essential care to start labor. In the hopes that the body would reject the dead, decomposing fetus, she advised Lita to carry the baby. After two weeks of anguish and discomfort, the couple tried to locate another ob-gyn for a second opinion. Doctors can resolve this rare condition only through termination.

Melencio then took her to a facility that performed surgical abortions. Lita was afraid of Melencio, so she followed him. They went to a midwife's house. The door opened reluctantly with a squeak. Their nose begins to fill with a musty, damp smell. The only sounds in the building were sporadic creaks and sighs. They entered a small, windowless office after following the old woman along a dreary hallway. The old woman's home also served as the clinic. Her sister, the practitioner, grinned as she welcomed them. They hurried to a dirty chamber, where Melencio helped his beloved settle into a bed that had a bloody odor.

"I'm sorry about this mess. I'm so used to it. I forget how it looks." The abortionist said.

Melencio did not respond. He could not focus as he was worried about his wife. The abortionist was an old woman in her sixties. She mentioned that she has done this many times, and couples were thankful for her skills. She then touched the belly of Lita.

"You're growing a unique individual in there." the old woman commented with surprising candor.

They asked Lita to sit on the bed, and she sobbed when they showed her the suction. Lita begged to go home. She gripped her husband's hand.

"Let's go home!" Lita pleaded.

Melencio felt pity for his wife and shoved the abortionist. The practitioner frowned and asked them to pay her. She angrily shouted that she needed the money. She smiled when Melencio handed him the money. They were yelled at by the abortionist, who was grinning, "You can't be parents; you are awful people!"

Melencio ignored the old woman, brought his wife home, and decided to keep the unborn baby.

He suddenly had a change of heart. He is ready to take care of a child with abnormalities. Lita appreciated that decision. That was one of the few times she felt good about her husband.

Lita lost all memory of previous events as soon as the midwife informed them that the newborn had already passed away during delivery. She realized that she had recently given birth to a dead child.

She cried out of pain. However, her tears multiplied when doctors informed her that she wouldn't be able to become pregnant anymore due to the damage to her uterus. Melencio underwent a significant transformation as a result of his anger over this. He stopped speaking with his significant other. The passion in his eyes was gone. The bed became empty, and they seemed to have been married for decades. He began to behave violently and became abusive to his wife.

Act 5: Lost and Found

The couple Melencio and Lita are fighting again. Every night, this has been a familiar scenario since they learned that Lita can no longer bear a child. Bruises cover Lita's face, and hand marks are visible on her wrists.

"I thought I asked for chicken soup today!" Melencio shouts. "You're so useless! I can't believe I even decided to marry you!"

The wife cried and stepped out of the house. She was holding onto her bloodied lips, which the abusive Melencio hit. She ran towards the woods, and Melencio followed her. No one knows what he is up to. There is aggression, and you can feel the tension in the air. The chase is short-lived. He caught his wife by her hair as she tried to escape.

However, her attempt to escape is entirely in vain. Melencio was muscular and too strong for the feminine Lita.

"Let me go!" Lita exclaimed.

"Come here!" shouted Melencio.

Then they heard an infant's cry. They stopped and traced the noise's origin until they reached a bamboo thicket, behind which was a beautiful baby.

They had longed for a baby, and now their prayers were answered. Lita took the baby in her arms while Melencio looked around to see if anyone else was around. He became assured that they were by themselves that night.

"Who would leave a beautiful baby here in the forest?" Lita asked.

"Only heartless souls can do that!" Melencio remarked. "Let's go back home!"

Act 6: The Trickery Begins

The couple cared for the baby for the next few days, feeding it, changing its diaper, and playing with it. Their feelings were confusion, apprehension, and an odd sense of responsibility. Lita, still reeling from the loss of her baby, felt a strange connection to the baby. She saw it as a chance to nurture something again, to give love and receive it in return. But simultaneously, she was unsure of the baby's strange behavior around her. The way it uncontrollably cried whenever she was near and seemed almost to taunt her with its laughter when she was feeling low made her feel disturbed and oddly drawn to the creature.

Melencio, on the other hand, mainly felt indifference towards the baby. To him, it was just another mouth to feed. He cared for it dutifully, feeding it and changing its diapers, but he didn't feel any emotional connection to it as Lita did. He's doing all these things to somehow make it up to his wife, who emotionally suffered when they lost their baby during pregnancy. Deep inside, he acknowledges that he is to blame for that tragedy.

Nonetheless, something was off with the baby; he couldn't understand why the baby cried so much around his wife, making him uneasy.

Despite their differing feelings towards the baby and their conflict, the couple worked together to care for it. They tried to ignore the strange behavior, chalking it up to the baby being abandoned alone in the forest or maybe just adjusting to its new surroundings. But deep down, they both knew that something was off. As the days went on, their unease grew more potent, and they couldn't shake the feeling that the infant they had taken into their home was manipulating them.

"Have you noticed the baby stops crying when you hold it?" Lita asked Melencio one day.

Melencio shrugged. "Maybe it just likes me better," he said, smiling at the baby.

Lita didn't look convinced. "It's strange, don't you think? Maybe we should take it to the hospital and get it checked out."

"No, it's fine," Melencio replied sharply, looking at Lita with annoyance. "We can even barely cover our expenses, and we're still paying the balance of your hospital bill!" Melencio's temper flared up as usual, "So, shut up! The baby is fine." dismissing Lita's concerns and walking out.

As the days passed, the baby's crying grew more intense whenever Lita was around. It was almost as if it could sense her pain and grief. Lita felt a strange connection to the baby, which comforted her in a way that nothing else could.

Lita's obsession with the baby grew stronger as the days went by. She spent all her time with the infant, neglecting her needs and responsibilities. She would sit for hours, just holding it, staring into its dark, unblinking eyes, feeling a strange sense of comfort in its presence.

Melencio became increasingly angry with Lita's obsession with the baby. He tried to talk some sense into her, reminding her that the baby was not their natural child, but Lita refused to listen. His anger boiled over, and he lashed out at Lita, yelling at her and even grabbing her by the arm in frustration. He raised his arm to slap Lita but stopped mid-way when he noticed Lita did not flinch. The blank expression on his wife's face took him aback.

"What the hell is going on, Lita?" he asked, trying to keep his voice calm, yet you could hear the anger taking shape.

"I can't let anyone take the baby away from me," Lita replied, her voice barely above a whisper. "It's mine, and I won't let anyone take it away."

Melencio felt a chill run down his spine. He had never seen Lita like this before. She had always been a loving and caring person, but now she seemed consumed by the baby's hold on her.

"You're scaring me, Lita," Melencio said, stepping closer to her. "Have you lost your mind? Let's give that child to the authority,"

Lita shook her head. "No, we can't give it up. We can't let anyone take it away. It's ours."

Act 7: Slowly Unraveling

Strange occurrences started happening around the house. At first, it was just small things like objects being moved from their usual place or doors opening and closing on their own. However, as time passed, the events became more and more bizarre.

One night, Lita suddenly woke up to check on the baby. She suddenly screamed in shock because the baby was not in the crib. Melencio was awoken by this, who was sleeping beside her in the bed. Lita looked around the room and then into the house. Melencio did the same, but his search was less extensive or enthusiastic than Lita's. Lita noticed this and began to suspect that her husband had a hand in the baby's disappearance.

"Where did you take the baby?" Lita shoved Melencio with all her force.

Melencio was caught out of balance and tumbled to the dish rack. The plates and utensils fell to the ground, wounding Melencio.

"Bitch!" Melencio stood up, notwithstanding his blood-stained white shirt because of his numerous wounds. He slapped Lita; he was furious. He intended to slap her again when he noticed Lita had taken one of the kitchen knives, so he slowly stepped back.

That's when they heard the baby crying. Hearing this, Lita suddenly threw the knife to the ground and followed the baby's crying sound. They found the baby under their bed. It was inconceivable how the baby could climb out of the crib and crawl under the bed. However, due to the tension and animosity between the couple, they did not talk about it and just slept separately.

That very next night, "Did you hear that, Melencio?" Lita whispered, her voice echoing concern.

Melencio hesitatingly raised his head from the pillow and listened closely. Sure enough, he heard the faint sound of a baby's cry. They hurriedly checked on the baby in his crib, but the baby slept soundly.

"That's impossible," he said, his voice barely above a whisper. "The baby is asleep." Melencio told himself.

Act 8: The Terror Intensifies

The incidents in the past few days made Melencio think about the baby a lot. They had always suspected something was not quite right with his baby since they found it in the woods. They had noticed odd behaviors, like the baby staring intently at nothing or crying inconsolably for no apparent reason. He also took note of the frequent physical and emotional confrontations between him and his wife and how they tend to increase not only in frequency but also in severity. He kept on trying to convince Lita to give it to the authorities so that they could find the actual parents of the infant. He even pleaded and appealed to her emotions as a parent; he told her about the distress that the mother of the baby was feeling looking for her baby. But nothing worked; Lita is so absorbed in the baby that she hardly notices anything else.

He sighed and shook his head in exasperation.

He went to drink with his buddies that night and came home intoxicated. Melencio walked slowly and silently so as not to wake his wife and the baby in the crib. He sat on the sofa in the sala and took one more bottle of gin from the fridge. He probably had more alcohol than he could take, yet he downed one more bottle.

Suddenly, he heard a commotion outside and went to investigate. As he peered through the window, he saw the neighbor's cat darting across the yard with the baby in hot pursuit. His eyes widened, and he was so shocked he could not speak. His mouth was agape, but no voice came out.

When he finally came around, he raced outside, calling out to the baby, but when he caught up, a horrifying sight met him.

The transformation was slow and subtle, but Melencio couldn't tear his eyes away. He watched in horror as his innocent baby's physical appearance began to change, morphing into something decidedly inhuman.

At first, it was just a subtle shifting of the baby's features. His once-round face became elongated, and his eyes took on a reddish glow. His tiny fingers grew long and slender, ending in razor-sharp claws that glinted in the room's dim light.

The transformation continued, and Melencio watched in horror as his baby's skin began to darken, taking on a sickly grey hue. His once-cute nose twisted and elongated, forming a snout filled with rows of razor-sharp teeth.

As the transformation reached its climax, the baby's body began to convulse, writhing and twisting as though it were in immense pain. Melencio wanted to look away, to shield his eyes from the horrifying scene before him, but he couldn't. Fear and probably alcohol paralyzed him, leaving him unable to do anything but watch as the baby transformed into a creature straight out of a nightmare.

Finally, the transformation was complete, and what had once been his baby now stood before him, a tiyanak, and its eyes blazing with an evil light.

Melencio watched in horror as the tiyanak sank its teeth into the cat, tearing flesh from bone.

That's when the tiyanak set its eye on Melencio. Melencio trembled with fear and disbelief. He couldn't move, couldn't even breathe, as he stared at the creature that had once been his adopted child. He knew he had to protect his wife from the monster inhabiting their home, but fear froze him.

The tiyanak hissed, and Melencio realized with a jolt that it was hungry. He tried to run, to escape the horror that had taken over his home, but the tiyanak was too fast. It lunged at him, its claws extended.

Melencio's body convulsed as the tiyanak's claws dug into his flesh, tearing at his skin with a sickening, squelching sound. Blood spattered the walls and floor, creating a gruesome scene that seemed to belong in a horror movie.

Melencio tried to scream, but the tiyanak had already sunk its razor-sharp teeth into his neck, cutting off his air supply. He gasped for breath, feeling his life slipping away as the creature continued to feast on his flesh.

His vision grew blurry, and he felt a sudden numbness spreading through his body. He knew that he was dying, that there was no escape from the tiyanak's deadly grip.

As he dropped to the floor, his body twitching and writhing in the throes of death, Melencio felt a sense of overwhelming regret. He shouldn't have ignored the red flags about this baby. But it was too late now. Melencio's lifeless body lay on the ground, his blood pooling around him as the tiyanak continued to feast on his remains.

Lita's eyes slowly opened as she woke up to an empty bed. She turned to her side and reached out to touch Melencio but felt only cold sheets. She called out to him, but there was no response.

"Strange, what could he be up to now?" she whispered.

She quickly got out of bed and rushed to the baby's room. The baby was sound asleep in the crib, but Melencio was also not there.

She walked over to the crib and gently touched the baby's forehead. The baby stirred but didn't wake up. Lita's heart sank as she noticed something strange. There was a dark substance smeared on the baby's face and all over its body, and Melencio's shirt lay crumpled on the floor next to the crib. She remembered that this was Melencio's shirt when he slept. She picked it up, and her eyes widened when she noticed the same brown substance the baby had all over its body and face. Not only that, but the shirt also looks like it was ripped apart. She tried to smell the shirt; she was sure the brown substance was dried blood. She was hysterical. She doesn't know what to think or how to process this information. Her heart was racing while trying to make sense of it all. Her breaths came in short gasps as she tried to process what was happening. Her heart pounded in her chest, and tears rose in her eyes.

"Melencio, Melencio," she blurted out in panic.

Lita quickly scooped up the baby, cradling it in her arms. She checked for any injuries, but the baby seemed utterly unharmed. She turned to leave the room, clutching the baby tightly to her chest.

Walking down the hallway, she noticed something strange on the floor. It was a trail of dark smears leading out of the house and into the darkness outside.

Lita's hands shook as she clutched the baby closer. She knew she needed to find Melencio, figure out what had happened, and act fast.

Suddenly, she heard a strange sound behind her. She turned around, and her eyes widened in horror as she saw the baby that she was holding staring back at her with glowing red eyes.

Lita stumbled back, dropping the baby in her panic, her heart racing with fear as the baby transformed before her very eyes into a full-grown tiyanak. Its fangs bared, and it advanced toward her with bloodlust in its eyes.

Its razor-sharp teeth sank into her shoulder, and Lita screamed in pain. Lita tried to fight back, but the tiyanak was too strong. As the tiyanak continued to attack, Lita's body weakened, and she felt lightheaded. Lita knew that she was losing too much blood. Tears streamed down Lita's face as she looked at the monstrous baby eagerly chewing on her flesh. The tiyanak's bloodlust intensified as it savored the taste of Lita's blood. It continued to attack, tearing into her flesh with wanton abandon. Lita's vision began to blur, and her body went limp.

With a final satisfied growl, the tiyanak dropped Lita's body to the ground and turned its attention to the couple's nearest neighbor. Once at the neighbor's yard, it transformed into a helpless baby and waited.

Act 9: The Aftermath

The sun rose when the neighbor stepped onto their porch and noticed something odd in their yard. As they approached, they realized that it was a baby lying on the ground, covered in what appeared to be dried blood.

Panic set in as the neighbors rushed over to the baby, their hearts racing as they quickly checked for any signs of life. The baby was breathing but appeared to be in shock. The neighbor frantically looked around, figuring out where the baby could have come from.

That's when they saw the blood trail leading into the dense foliage surrounding their neighborhood. The neighbor followed the trail, feeling a sense of dread growing in their chest with each step.

They went through the foliage when the neighbor's worst fears became reality. There, hidden in the underbrush, was the half-eaten body of Melencio. The neighbor stumbled back in horror, barely managing to hold back the urge to vomit.

The neighbor stumbled further into the brush, feeling a sickening dread as they searched for Lita. It didn't take long to find her, her body just a few feet away from Melencio's.

She, too, had been attacked and left to die.

The following day, the neighbor who had found the baby called the police to report the gruesome discovery of Melencio and Lita's half-eaten bodies in the dense foliage near their neighborhood. The police arrived on the scene, and the neighbor led them to where he had found the bodies.

One of the officers approached the neighbor and asked, "Did you see or hear anything suspicious last night?"

The neighbor shook his head. "No, I was sound asleep when I found the baby this morning. But something strange has been happening in the neighborhood lately. People have been hearing strange noises at night, and there have been reports of missing pets."

The officer nodded, taking note of the neighbor's information. "We'll investigate this further. For now, we need to take the bodies for further investigation."

The neighbor watched as the police carefully lifted the bodies of Melencio and Lita onto stretchers and placed them into their van. He couldn't believe something like this could happen in their quiet neighborhood.

As the police were leaving, the neighbor remembered something and called out to them. "Wait! There's something else you should know. Melencio and Lita have a baby; I found it this morning."

The officer turned back and asked, "Where is the baby now?"

"It's in my house. I took care of it while waiting for you to arrive."

The officer nodded. "We'll need to take the baby into our custody for now. We'll contact the proper authorities and have it put up for adoption."

The police officers carefully lifted the baby from the neighbor's arms, gently placing it into a car seat. The neighbor watched on, a mixture of shock and sadness across her face.

"I can't believe it," she murmured, tears threatening to spill over.

"I know," one of the officers replied, "It's a tragic situation for everyone involved."

"But what about the baby?" the neighbor asked, "What will happen to it now?"

"We're going to take it to the hospital, make sure doctors check it over and provide any necessary medical treatment. Then, we'll place it with a loving family that can provide a safe and secure home."

The officers closed the doors to the car, the baby's cries growing softer as they drove away. The neighbor watched them go.

Epilogue

As an old lady stopped mixing the casserole, the scent of freshly cooked food permeated the macabre kitchen. Using the same spoon, she took a sip of the gory soup. Satisfied with what she had tasted, she took a piece of the smoky meat and chewed a portion. She then removed something stuck on her teeth, a soft nail from one of the fingers of the fetus that she had just cooked.

The cook then started serving the food to the table and called her masters for dinner. The head of the house came to the table with his wife and started eating. They praised the servant for the baby soup. The old lady just watched the husband and wife enjoying the meal.

The cook was brought to the Philippines by her masters from their country. They belong to a Chinese ethnic group who believes that eating a fetus improves health and boosts sexual performance. The old lady has served the Chinese family for more than five decades after her parents sold her to them as a debt settlement.

She was cleaning the kitchen sink when she heard a baby's cry from outside. Curiosity got the best of her, and she got up and approached where the noise was coming from. The infant's crying became louder as the servant got nearer.

There was a baby on the porch; someone must have left it there, she thought to herself. She picked it up slowly while looking around for anyone who had left it there. It is not uncommon for depressed parents to leave their infant at the front door of well-to-do people in the hope of giving their child a better future. There was no one around as she scanned the surroundings. After ensuring they were all alone, she focused on the child.

Her eyes lit up. The baby was so cute. She held the baby's legs and gently patted the muscles on the hands and legs. She noted how plump and tender the meat was. The baby innocently smiled at her. She grinned back.

She carried the baby to the kitchen and looked for the chopping board and meat cleaver. Unbeknownst to her, the baby she was holding started to twitch and shake violently. She remembered that she had left the meat cleaver on the front porch. She carefully made her way there, taking tiny steps not to bump anything because the light was already off and dark.

The baby slowly transformed. Its soft, small ears turned into long, pointed ears. Its little eyes turned into large, sneering eyes, and its lips grinned a devilish smile that slowly revealed its razor-sharp fangs.

The old woman cried out in pain and agony as the tiny creature bit a huge chunk of her neck. Her blood immediately sprayed out of her jugular. In no time, her vision went dark due to blood loss. The creature devoured her in a feeding frenzy. The old woman was now dead at this point; her stomach was split open, and her internal organs protruded. The Tiyanak continued to extract her internal organs before eating them.

-The End-

In a quiet, seemingly peaceful neighborhood, a horrific discovery shatters the calm when a baby is found alone, covered in blood, leading to the gruesome remains of its parents. But as the police attempt to make sense of the tragedy, a more profound, darker secret begins to unfold. What starts as an act of kindness quickly becomes a nightmare when the child's true nature reveals itself.—a creature born from Filipino folklore with an insatiable hunger for flesh. As terror takes hold, no one is safe from the ancient evil that has awakened.

Written by
Jayson R. Valencia
Rodulfo Q. Todio

JAYSON R. VALENCIA
RODULFO Q. TODIO

THE GUMIHO
OF THE
GOTJAWAL FOREST

Her smile hides fangs, and her love demands blood.

The Gumiho of the Gotjawal Forest

An ancient evil awakens in the heart of Jeju Island's Gotjawal Forest. When Hyun-Woo's wife, Ha-eun, battles the demons of postpartum depression after a tragic miscarriage, she unwittingly invites a sinister force into their lives—a mysterious girl whose arrival stirs buried fears and dark desires. As Ha-eun finds fleeting solace in her new "daughter," Hyun-Woo's nightmares intensify, revealing a chilling premonition of death. In a tale steeped in folklore and blood, the boundaries of motherhood and monstrosity blur, leading to a horrifying revelation that may cost them their lives.
Her smile hides fangs, and her love demands blood.

Introduction

The broken window reflected Ha-eun crouching next to the toilet bowl, her tangled black hair drenched in tears. There was blood on her face. The fractured mirror might have injured her flesh. There was a mess of toiletries on the floor. She was examining her wrist while holding a razor-sharp blade. She's been disregarding me. She looked at me outside the lone bathroom window as I pleaded with her to stop what she was thinking of doing. My pleading fell on deaf ears as she proceeded to slice her wrist. Blood spilled out like a hose and gushed to the floor.

Her husband arrived and forced the door open. He carried his unconscious wife out of the bathroom. I called the ambulance, and we arrived at the nearest hospital after a few minutes.

Hyun-Woo and I waited at the entrance of the emergency room.

I was working as a yeoja ileum, or a nanny, in South Korea when I witnessed a bloody suicide scene. My boss, Ha-eun, locked herself in the restroom for hours after having a miscarriage and finding out that she couldn't have a baby anymore. I called her husband, Hyun-Woo, who was at work, to ask him to go home immediately. I could hear Ha-eun crying until she became silent inside the hwajangshil. I kept knocking at the door to no avail. I looked at the lone high window, took a stainless ladder, and peered through the changmun.

Ha-eun passed out after losing too much blood. Blood covered the toilet, resembling red paint on a canvas. Hyun-Woo arrived and rescued his wife. He applied direct pressure and bandages to stop the bleeding. Thankfully, the ambulance arrived on time.

Hyun-Woo has treated me like a family member. I cared for his father until someone murdered the old man. It was a tragedy that I have had difficulty coping with since I don't know anyone in my life except for Hyun-Woo's father. Then, Hyun-Woo took me to take care of his wife, who was having a difficult pregnancy. Hyun-Woo told me that he suspected terrible things would happen to his wife. He had nightmares of himself holding a shovel and burying his wife in the forest.

Act 1: Ha-eun Depression

The physicians managed to save Ha-Eun. She was diagnosed with postpartum depression because of her miscarried pregnancy. Her doctors also told her that she was incapable of getting pregnant ever again. Her depression deepened to the point that she feared everyone and everything, even me. During her usual panic attack, she usually cries that a nine-tailed fox is chasing after her. She was always sweating from head to toe, and her knees trembled during these episodes.

She was adamant that I should not go near her; she only wanted her husband to be with her and rejected me. Whenever I strayed near her, Ha-eun would glare at me, her eyes tense and worried, saying, "Stay away from me."

Hyun-Woo would come near and comfort her. I left them and went to the hospital's canteen to buy food. Hyun-Woo has not eaten anything since taking his wife to the hospital.

The doctor informed us that Ha-eun was out of danger. However, she suffered from depression since she had no chance of giving birth. Her state of mind is unstable. In most cases, she would mention the uncanny figure of a nine-tailed fox running after her. Soon, someone informed her husband of her possible insanity.

We returned to their house near the Gotjawal forest on Jeju Island to avoid people. His father purchased the land and lived here while suffering from a cerebral infarction. The father died there with his internal organs, particularly the liver, missing. The autopsy speculated that a savage animal did that to him. I have no recollection of what happened. They found me passed out and bloodied near the forest. Some said that I was dragged there by whatever killed Hyun-woo's father. From the looks of it, I will be its next meal, but something spared me for some unknown reason.

Their hanok is a typical Korean house with a mountain in the background and a river in front. It was a beautiful L-shaped house designed to withstand extreme temperatures during the summer and winter seasons. It has an ondol made of stone, an underfloor heating system, and a maru, a cooling system made of clay. I felt at home in this place since I took care of his father here for several years. His father found me in the forest and took me home, treating me as his own.

Hyun-Woo had nightmares since our arrival at the house on Jeju Island. It was disturbing him, so he told me about his nasty dreams. According to him, he was alone in the forest, digging the ground with a shovel. An outdoor lamp placed on the ground was the only source of light. Hyun-Woo was digging for his wife's tomb. He put the soil back in the hole to cover the corpse of his wife. Her eyes opened as the soil covered her chest. Hyun-Woo kept putting the soil back, covering the face of his wife.

Act 2: An Answered Prayer

Ha-eun's situation worsened. She mentioned to her husband that she had been having visions. According to her story, she saw a beautiful bride who had accidentally stripped off her clothes at a wedding. They revealed her actual appearance. She had a foxy face with upright ears and nine tails. She attacked and devoured all the guests. I just smiled upon hearing it and gave Hyun-Woo a bowl of kimchi soup. I asked him to feed his wife since she would not allow me to do so.

One day, Hyun-Woo was looking at the mountain when I approached him. He mentioned that the only way for his wife to heal was for her to bear a child. I told him that he could appease the Sanshin or mountain gods. I don't know much about my parents or upbringing because I was still a child when Hyn-Woo's father found me lost in the forest. He never saw my parents, despite his best efforts. I was surprised that I knew a lot of things about Sanshin. I believe my real family indoctrinated me about these things when I was a child.

"The mountain's beauty, mystery, and shape that soars toward the sky is your stairway to heaven," I said, wondering how I knew this. I also told him that the upper mountain slopes, cliffs, and summits are where one can speak with spirits, see visions, or experience enlightenment.

"A mountain connects the heavenly realm to the earth where humans reside?" he asked.

I answered, "Yes, it serves as a link between the two worlds," not knowing that my answer would result in a tragedy.

Hyun-Woo did not tell us that he would embark on a journey to Mt. Yeongsan to pray to the mountain gods to have a child. He left in the morning after feeding his wife. He went back in the afternoon, just before sunset. He was carrying a bloodied young girl with abdominal cramps. The girl had spots of red-brown discharge. I later found out that it was her first menstruation and realized that she was around twelve to thirteen years old. I was about the same age when Hyun-Woo's father found me.

She was a beautiful child he saw in the Gotjawal forest on his way to the mountain peak. He immediately came back home, feeling that something instantly answered his prayers. The girl had the slender features of a forest wolf and long, brown hair tinged with white. She doesn't talk but shows her emotions by grinning when happy and grimacing when disgusted. I cleaned her and gave her chamomile tea to relieve her menstrual cramps.

Act 3: Almost Cured

The moment that Ha-eun saw the young girl, she smiled. That was her first smile after her attempted suicide. She looked at the child, touched her hands, and embraced her. The child smiled, too, but her eyes hid an evil intention. I could tell that she was hiding something nasty in her eyes.

Ha-eun was happy and virtually healed when her husband showed her what the "gods" had given them. The young girl acted strangely. She was not talking. She was awake the whole night and slept in the morning. Ha-eun would look at her, touch her hair, and cuddle her.

But soon, strange things happen at the house. There was a chilling shriek at night. Then, our Maltese dog gave birth to a lone puppy, and the puppy died. The mother dog ate her puppy. The child and I witnessed it. After a few days, I smelled rotten meat and traced its source. I traced it under vintage furniture. Our Maltese dog was lifeless and covered in blood. The body was ripped open. The same happened with our kosher cat. She was just lying in our yard with her blood scattered all over. The next day, the chickens and goats were also slit open. Hyun-Woo and Ha-eun did not care at all. Hyun-Woo was more focused on his wife's recovery, while Ha-eun was still ecstatic at the presence of her new child.

Act 4: The Gumiho

After a few days, some of our neighbors reported that a predator killed their livestock and ripped their bodies open. Fear engulfed the village. They saw a fox-like creature strolling at night among the widely scattered houses. I felt a sharp pain in my temple upon hearing this. The pain gradually spread all over my head.

I realize I have been lacking sleep since the young girl arrived in the last few days. She was awake all night and would doze off in the morning. I also noticed that she was seducing Hyun-Woo. Compared to the typical adolescent, she had accelerated physical development. She had larger breasts than the majority of young girls. Although she did not talk, I could see her holding Hyun-Woo's hands, enticing him maliciously.

I woke up one night in a cold sweat despite the usual cold temperature outside. I was panting and agitated. I shook the feeling off and got a whiff of a familiar scent. I can't describe it. I can't even remember how it became familiar, but it prompted me to trace the smell silently.

The night was chilly and dark when I slowly crept out our back door. Somehow, my instinct tells me not to expose my body fully but to protrude my head from the opening of the door slightly. That's when I saw the young girl outside with only her sleeping clothes and barefoot. Like I was stalking her, she was stalking a man in his forties. The man was looking back and was walking at a hurried pace. He knew someone was following him, but he didn't realize that someone was a child.

I slowly stepped out of the door and followed the two. My heart was racing, and I felt I was operating on my heightened senses. Somehow, I knew the child was following the old man and hunting him like a fox. My eyes followed her as she ran in a steady-pace trotting gait. She crept within range and, without any hesitation, she pounced on her target from above. She ripped him open with her razor-sharp claws.

I was so shocked at the scene that I held my breath for a long time, perhaps longer than I should have. I made a choking noise while gasping for air.

I hid for a while, waiting for any clue that someone had discovered my position. But there were none. After a while, I finally got the courage to take another look.

The little girl was on top of the body as she devoured the old man's heart and liver.

At that time, panic sets in on me. I knew I needed to get out and return to the house as soon as possible. If not, I'll be the child's next meal. I took a deep breath as I thought about returning without being noticed. I was shivering. It seemed that the temperature had dropped even more. I could see my breath as a small cloud was released when I exhaled.

I confirmed at that point that the young girl did not have a menstrual discharge when Hyun-Woo found her. The blood was the blood of her victim, and she acted in pain to entice him. Then, I heard this loud howling sound. I turned, and standing behind me was this fox-like figure. It had piercing orange eyes that just looked through me. I tried to hide, and the next thing I knew, it was so close to my face that I could smell its breath. It had a bloody, raw, meaty odor. I could not breathe because its hands were so chilly and wrapped around me. I began to gasp for air as I struggled to get away from this situation. Its arms pressed harder, causing considerable discomfort for me. She grabbed my throat and pressed it hard. Suddenly, she halted abruptly and vanished from my line of sight.

When she was gone, I understood everything. The child revealed herself to me as a Gumiho. She shapeshifted into a child, aiming to devour as many human livers as possible to become human. There is a common belief that if I don't tell anyone about her in ten years, she will become a human. For some reason, I decided not to tell anyone.

Act 5: The Enlightenment

I was standing next to the river in front of the hanok. It was a full moon. The moon's reflection in the river gave me some enlightenment. I looked at the grassland and realized that the moon's light, despite its vastness and magnificence, was also mirrored in dewdrops on the grass. I touched the water in the river and shattered the reflection. Even the drops of water captured the light of the moon.

I started to have a clearer picture of my past. It was still hazy, but it sent shivers up my spine. It was a mix of emotions. I remembered how the young girl devoured the man's heart and liver. She consumed the man in an epicurean sense. My memory deceived me as I saw myself replacing the girl. I was devouring the man. Blood was drooling from my mouth. My eyes were shining brightly with delight.

Suddenly, my recollection of my past was interrupted when I heard a loud, chilling shriek inside the house. I ran as quickly as possible, and when I reached there, the Gumiho had already killed Hyun-Woo. I saw her on top of his back. Blood coated Hyun-Woo. He was lying on the floor facing down. The Gumiho has broken his spine and back ribs. She had ripped him open and was consuming his liver. The sight was familiar and gave me some satisfaction. I drooled as I remembered the meat's sweet taste and soft texture. However, when I turned to my right, I was shocked that Ha-eun also saw it. She was standing still in the corner of the room.

I was so confused. Ha-eun already knew that her child was a Gumiho. Could she love the child so much that she is determined to help her eat all the human livers she needs to become human, even that of her husband?

When the Gumiho was satisfied, she returned to her room and locked herself in. Ha-eun asked me to clean up the mess nonchalantly. I buried Hyun-Woo in the backyard using a trenching shovel. I wrapped his body in a blanket and dropped it into a pit I dug. I was emotionless as I covered him with soil.

I recalled how the Gumiho devoured Hyun-Woo. He looked like his father, who died the same way. I also remembered Hyun-Woo's suspicion that he would bury his wife with a shovel. Similar events also flashed in my mind. It was as if it wasn't my first time burying a dead person.

Neighbors knocked on the door the next day and asked for Hyun-Woo's whereabouts. Two were bearded but balding, while the third was nearly obese. Ha-eun became agitated and asked me to drive them away. The Gumiho peered out from her door.

The men wanted to discuss with me the series of killings in the village. The men left when Ha-eun shouted at them. That night, Ha-eun asked me to help the Gumiho hunt the men. The men placed a net trap that caught the young girl, but Ha-eun freed her. She attacked each one of them with her razor-sharp claws. She beheaded the two while Haeun hit the third one with a shovel. The Gumiho feasted on the livers of the three. However, in her rage and perhaps because she was still not satisfied. The Gumiho jumped on Ha-eun and slaughtered her. I have no time to react. I just realized what happened when Ha-eun was already sprawled on the ground while the little girl was feasting on her. Her demise confirmed her husband's foreboding that he would be responsible for his wife's death. Ha-eun's death made me recall everything from my past.

The residents of the town will soon come. They knew I buried Hyun-Woo. They will come not only for the head of the Gumiho but also for mine. As a former Gumiho, I became a human after eating the liver of Hyun-Woo's father. I have to run and get back to the forest. But before that, I will kill the girl, cut her open, and take the fox bead inside her. The fox beads, a source of life and energy, will sustain my mortal life and allow me to live eternally.

I will lurk in the Gotjawal forest, waiting for someone to ravage.

-The End-

An ancient evil awakens in the heart of Jeju Island's Gotjawal Forest. When Hyun-Woo's wife, Ha-eun, battles the demons of postpartum depression after a tragic miscarriage, she unwittingly invites a sinister force into their lives—a mysterious girl whose arrival stirs buried fears and dark desires. As Ha-eun finds fleeting solace in her new "daughter," Hyun-Woo's nightmares intensify, revealing a chilling premonition of death. In a tale steeped in folklore and blood, the boundaries of motherhood and monstrosity blur, leading to a horrifying revelation that may cost them their lives.

Written by

Jayson R. Valencia
Rodulfo Q. Todio

Jayson R. Valencia
Rodulfo Q. Todio
From the depths of despair, a vengeful spirit awakens.
Tyanak's Revenge

Tyanak's Revenge

In the upscale suburbs of Manila, Leni's life spirals into chaos as she grapples with a difficult pregnancy, haunted by a past love and the specter of loss. As she navigates the pressures of family expectations and her emotional turmoil, an evil force lurks within her—a Tiyanak, a vengeful spirit that craves blood and destruction. When the nightmare manifests into reality during a hospital stay, Leni must confront not only her demons but also a terrifying creature that threatens to consume everything she holds dear. With each chilling twist, Tiyanak's Terror explores the dark intersections of love, betrayal, and the supernatural, leading to a shocking conclusion that will leave readers breathless.

From the depths of despair, a vengeful spirit awakens. This time, there will be no escape.

Prologue

The hospital door flew open to the frantic sound of an ambulance siren. Yaya Imelda, the longtime house helper of the Bongbong and Leni couple, rushed alongside the corridor to follow the rolling stretcher of her Madame. Leni was unconscious; her cream cotton skirt was drenched with blood because she had a miscarriage.

Mang Isko, the couple's longtime driver, is closely following. He has been on call for nearly thirty minutes, updating Bongbong on his wife's situation. His boss was on a business trip when all of this happened. Bongbong told Mang Isko that he had already cut his business trip and was now rushing to the hospital.

A tense situation unfolded in the urgent care unit, where medical staff treated other people for wounds caused by car collisions, gunshot wounds, and other mishaps. The patients were either crying or grimacing in pain, while the others were staring blankly at the wall.

"God help my Madame," Yaya Imelda whispered.

Yaya Imelda glanced to the right, where she could see other pregnant moms lined up in the birthing section, which was on the second level of the building, via the open large windows. Some were on the bed, while others were standing. Despite being a private hospital, the expectant mothers were too many to be handled by the hospital.

Act 1: A Difficult Pregnancy

Leni and Bongbong are from well-to-do families in Manila, the Philippines' capital. Their parents are business partners and have pre-arranged their marriage.

Their black Mercedes Benz had just parked in the garage after passing through the automated gate. The driver attempted to assist Leni after opening the vehicle door.

"I'll take care of it, Mang Isko." Bongbong took his wife's hand and led her into their custom-built home in the upscale suburb. It's a five-bedroom, five-bathroom house with a swimming pool in the front yard.

"We'll have to recruit another maid to assist Yaya Imelda." Leni expressed her thoughts.

Yaya Imelda quickly responded that she could take care of herself and clean the house since their parents also sent some helpers to clean the house on weekends. "Do you want to eat anything?" the 50-year-old woman asked.

"I would rather sleep, I'm tired," Leni responded.

Bongbong interrupted, "But you haven't eaten anything." Then, turning to their nanny, he said, "Yaya, just bring her a glass of warm milk."

"I don't want to drink milk." Leni held her stomach and opened her mouth, indicating that she was in pain.

"What happened?" asked her husband, who was very worried. "Do you want me to call a doctor?"

Leni did not reply and sat on the sofa in their living room. She was in her second trimester of pregnancy, but her condition was as tricky as the first. She vomits every morning and sometimes suffers from constipation and minor fever.

Mang Isko appeared and asked, "Sir, should I call the doctor now?" He was holding a cell phone that his boss, Bongbong, had given him as a bonus last Christmas.

"I'm good Mang Isko." Leni stated as she rested her head on the pillow.

Yaya Imelda came with a glass of milk and placed it on the center table.

Bongbong reached for the glass of milk he offered Leni, but she shoved him, causing the glass to slide from his grip and fall to the floor.

They heard the crackling of shattered glass and saw poured milk on the floor.

"I told you I don't want milk," Leni said, annoyed.

Mang Isko immediately scooped up the shattered glass while Yaya Imelda cleaned it with a mop and a dustpan.

Bongbong got up and went into the main bedroom, shaking his head.

Act 2: A Haunting Memory

Leni fell asleep on the sofa and had a nightmare. She was taken to an abortion clinic by her parents, and she was shouting in pain. Her two legs were open as she lay on a stingy bed. The abortionist was holding a metal forceps, and then he inserted it into her vagina.

She screamed in pain, and a man entered the room to save her. She awoke at that point.

Rodrigo, her first love, was the man in her dream, not Bongbong. She recalled his gaze and lips, as well as their shared experiences. She smiled as she remembered how they met at the mall and dated without her parent's knowledge.

When she remembered the day her parents found out about their affair, her pleasure changed to sadness. She was confined to her room and barred from seeing Rodrigo. She assumed that if they had a child, her parents would embrace Rodrigo, but they still rejected him because her parents had betrothed her to their business partner's son.

Rodrigo died in a motorbike accident, Leni discovered afterward. At first, she believed her parents were involved, but she changed her mind after they explained that it was all an accident. Leni's world flipped upside down, and she didn't eat for a week until doctors hospitalized her.

When she recovered, her parents pressured Leni to get an abortion, which was illegal in their country, so they had to settle for a clandestine abortion facility.

Act 3: The Unhappy Wife

Leni's parents force her to marry Bongbong. She could not resist them, for they threatened her that she wouldn't be a part of their last will. Since Rodrigo was dead, Leni agreed but never showed affection to her husband.

Bongbong, on the other hand, loved Leni at first sight. When he escorted her on her debut or 18th birthday, he met her for the first time. He'll never forget how stunning she looked in her red gown. They also danced that night in the function ballroom of the Diamond Hotel, where they held the event. His first and last dance with a lady was that one.

Bongbong has given Leni his whole attention. Despite the presence of their nanny, Bongbong was the one who prepared her slippers and bathtub and even learned to cook for her, even though he had not done these things while he was still a single guy since they were wealthy.

He bought new baby clothes, diapers, and milk and asked Mang Isko to put them in his office. Then he motioned for Leni to enter the office, bringing her in with his arm on Leni's shoulders.

Bongbong opened the door, expecting his wife to be happy and surprised.

Leni's face was expressionless. She grimaced when she saw the clothing he bought.

She commented, "Why would you buy boy's clothing when we don't know the gender yet?"

"I could just buy another set of baby clothing in case we have a girl," he said as Bongbong expressed regret.

"I always wished for a little daughter, not a boy!" Leni remarked as she clasped her hands around her waist.

"All right, and here's the milk and diapers for our baby girl," Bongbong stated tenderly. "I simply followed my father's advice because they expect a grandson."

"There you go, Bong," Leni said, her face red with annoyance. "You always defer to your parents' decisions."

"However-" Bongbong paused his discourse when Leni turned away and returned to her bed.

Bongbong sat on his chair, staring at the baby's clothes. He grasped them and shook his head, tears filling his eyes.

Leni had another nightmare. This time, a man wearing jeans and a jacket with a black hood was trying to hurt her. She ran as fast as she could in the street, but the man chased her. When she stumbled on a gutter on the road, she fell and saw the man approaching him. He removed his hood, and he saw that it was Rodrigo.

Bongbong shook her shoulder and said, "Wake up, you were screaming."

Act 4: Delusions or Real Phantom

Bongbong was on a week-long business trip. Leni lay on her bed with so many things on her mind. She tried to sleep but was unable to do so. She pushed herself into a sitting position and grabbed the glass of water Yaya Imelda had prepared for her earlier at night.

At this moment, out of the corner of her eyes, she noticed a shadow moving towards her. The closer the shadow gets, the dimmer the night lamp beside her becomes. She was shaking in fear and frantically called Yaya Imelda and Mang Isko.

Leni was in vertigo, as if her room was spinning around her. Alongside this, she also hears Rodrigo screaming at her. She also saw a vision of Rodrigo shouting something and pointing towards her belly. She interpreted this as being cursed because she had not tried to verify the truth behind Rodrigo's demise.

Leni felt a sharp pain in her belly. "O my God! My baby!" Her eyes widened with concern. The pain was unbearable. She could see her belly moving eerily as if the baby was clawing himself out. It was at this point that she fainted.

The hospital door flew open to the frantic sound of an ambulance siren. Yaya Imelda rushed alongside the corridor to follow the rolling stretcher of her Madame. Leni was unconscious; her cream cotton skirt was drenched with blood because she had a miscarriage.

Mang Isko is closely following. He has been on call for nearly thirty minutes and is now updating Bongbong about his wife's situation. His boss was on a business trip when all of this happened. Bongbong told Mang Isko that he had already cut his business trip and was now rushing to the hospital.

Leni woke up at the hospital with Yaya Imelda and Mang Isko on her side.

"Ma'am. Don't move. I'll call the doctor," Yaya Imelda said, immediately leaving the room.

Mang Isko told her that her husband was on the way to the hospital.

When he immediately checked on his wife, who was now asleep. The physician told him that Leni had a miscarriage and that they removed the dead baby. They currently placed their baby's body in the morgue.

Bongbong covered his face and wept like he never wept before.

Act 5: The Final Warning

For a long time now, Rodrigo has been trying to warn the love of his life about the demonic entity called Tiyanak that has taken over her baby in her womb. The baby has long died in the earlier stage of her pregnancy. But Leni's hatred of her husband, Bongbong, and her parents, which she blamed for the death of her one true love, Rodrigo, opened the dead body of the fetus for possession by demonic forces.

Rodrigo tried to appear in Leni's dream, physical manifestation through the shadows and other electrical equipment in her room. Still, Leni's hate kept growing, thereby feeding the demonic entity in her womb.

In Rodrigo's desperation, he tries to warn Leni one last time about her impending doom and those around her. He will do this by possession of the only living thing inside Leni's hospital room.

Rodrigo took possession of the lone mosquito in Leni's room. He maneuvered the mosquito behind Leni's ear just slightly above her face. She was sleeping deeply at that time, still recuperating from her miscarriage.

And from there, he opened his heart to her. With deep sadness and regret, he mentioned that he loved her and would love her for eternity. He regrets falling into the trap that her parents prepared for him. He told her that her parents poisoned him and he died in a motorbike accident on the way to the hospital. Most importantly, he told her about the danger of the Tiyanak, who was now out of her body. This demonic entity will surely go after her and will consume her flesh.

Leni suddenly woke up to the irritating noise; she slapped the pesky insect near her ear.

"Annoying bastard!" she murmured as she stood up to wash off the dead mosquito in her face and hands in the bathroom.

Act 6: Let Leni Live

On the second night of Leni's hospital stay, she suddenly woke up in a commotion outside her room in the corridor. She scanned the room and saw that Bongbong was sleeping, sitting on a chair beside her bed. She suddenly felt compassion for Bongbong for all the pain and rejection that she had subjected him to.

Yaya Imelda and Mang Isko slept on different chairs in the far corner of her room. She was ready to wake up when she noticed them moving and realized the bustle outside their hospital room was getting louder.

She gently nudged her husband, Bongbong, "Honey, wake up." It was the first time she had called Bongbong a term of endearment. Bongbong opened his eyes and could not believe what he heard. He was about to ask if he heard his wife calling him "honey" when shouting and crying jolted everyone in the room from the hospital corridor.

"Merciful Lord!" Yaya Imelda said as she made the sign of the cross.

"What's happening?" Mang Isko asked, confused from suddenly waking up.

Bongbong stood up and looked at Leni, "Don't worry, I'll check what's happening." He walked towards the door.

It suddenly flung open a few steps before he could reach the door. A nurse told them that a vicious animal was inside the hospital and was attacking people. She told them to stay inside their room. Then, she hurriedly closed the door and ran to her station.

They could not believe what they heard. After a few more minutes, the commotion and shouting crescendoed. Leni covered her ears. Mang Isko went to the toilet and held the metal curtain bar when he walked out. Bongbong looked at him and raised his eyebrow.

"Just for protection, sir," Mang Isko explained.

Yaya Imelda went to the other side of Leni's bed and held Leni's arm. "Don't worry, Ma'am". Leni nodded to her.

They are all looking at the door at this point. Then, suddenly, everything went silent in the corridor. They all looked at each other.

Not a minute later, they heard a baby crying at their door. Yaya Imelda immediately ran to the door and opened it, followed by Mang Isko, who was holding the metal bar at a ready.

"My God, Ma'am, Sir, It's a baby," Yaya Imelda picked it up from the floor.

"Who could have been this heartless to just leave a baby on the floor with a vicious animal around," Leni asked Bongbong. His husband did not answer.

"Take the baby and go inside quickly." Mang Isko told Yaya Imelda nervously.

Yaya Imelda picked up the baby in her arms and walked inside the room, after which Mang Isko promptly locked the door.

As soon as Yaya Imelda carried it near her shoulders, the infant suddenly bit a huge chunk of her neck. Yaya Imelda's blood sprayed from her neck into Mang Isko's face. Mang Isko fell on the floor in fright. Yaya Imelda's eyes went all white and turned pale from the blood loss.

She dropped dead, twitching. She even protected the infant from the fall.

Bongbong and Leni's eyes widened. Leni shouted Yaya Imelda's name; she was crying profusely. Yaya Imelda was more than a maid to her; she was the one who raised her from childhood.

When the infant suddenly stood up, Bongbong was about to run to Yaya Imelda's aid. This time, it doesn't look like an infant anymore. It looked more like a demon with sagging skin and a very flat nose. It took a single step; its movement is crooked due to its uneven legs. It looked at Bongbong with hate in its crimson eyes. It smiled, revealing sharp fangs and claws.

Bongbong moved back and decided to secure his wife, who was still crying in bed. He looked at Mang Isko and saw that the old man was too shocked to move.

"Mang Isko," Bongbong whispered to his driver.

Mang Isko came to his senses and looked at Bongbong.

"Come to us slowly," Bongbong instructed Mang Isko.

The creature looked at Mang Isko. It made ticking noises and jumped on the old man.

Mang Isko remembered the metal bar in his hand. He swung it at the creature and hit it in the forehead.

The creature reeled and ran to the toilet. Seeing this, Mang Isko stood up and instructed Bongbong to carry Leni.

"We're going out of here." Mang Isko told Bongbong and Leni while keeping his eyes on the toilet door.

Bongbong carried his wife in his arms and walked towards Mang Isko. Mang Isko opened the door for the couple, not taking his eyes off the creature's last location.

The couple walked a few steps and stopped.

Mang Isko noticed them looking at his back outside the opened door.

Hundreds of the same creatures are behind the door on the hospital corridor.

Epilogue

Ferdie and Cory, Leni's parents, were counting their money in the safe. Their fortune grew exponentially due to the help of their daughter's husband's family.

In their mind, they deserve this good fortune because they worked hard for it. They even have to kill their daughter's first boyfriend to make this happen.

Cory gave Ferdie a hot cup of coffee. Ferdie held the cup and took a sip.

"Perfect as always, my dear." Ferdie complimented Cory's coffee.

Cory smiled and looked at their front door.

"Did you hear that?" Cory asked Ferdie as she lowered the volume of their television.

"Yes, it's a baby crying, dear," Ferdie stood up and walked towards the door. "Oh my! It is a baby indeed." He picked it up.

Cory excitedly walked to the door to see. "It's so cute." She motioned Ferdie to carry it and sit on the couch. She checked outside to see if there was anyone there. After ensuring no one was around, she locked the door.

They both sat on the couch and adored the infant.

"How much can we get if we sell this baby?" Cory looked at Ferdie, grinning.

Ferdie did not get the chance to reply because the baby, who doesn't look like a baby anymore, clawed on his face continually. Blood splattered everywhere. Ferdie was convulsing and was in shock from his injuries.

Cory ran to the master's bedroom and immediately locked the door. Suddenly, she felt a sharp pain in her legs. When she looked, another demon child was chewing on her legs. She cried in pain and, most importantly, in fear because right behind the Tiyanak were hundreds more inside the room.

Blood splattered everywhere as the Tiyanaks devoured her.

-The End-

In the upscale suburbs of Manila, Leni's life spirals into chaos as she grapples with a difficult pregnancy, haunted by a past love and the specter of loss. As she navigates the pressures of family expectations and her emotional turmoil, an evil force lurks within her—a Tiyanak, a vengeful spirit that craves blood and destruction. When the nightmare manifests into reality during a hospital stay, Leni must confront not only her demons but also a terrifying creature that threatens to consume everything she holds dear. With each chilling twist, Tiyanak's Terror explores the dark intersections of love, betrayal, and the supernatural, leading to a shocking conclusion that will leave readers breathless.

Written by
Jayson R. Valencia
Rodulfo Q. Todio

Author Bio

Jayson R. Valencia and Rodulfo Q. Todio are renowned Filipino authors specializing in horror fiction with a flair for folklore. They have co-authored over 60 stories, including books like Tales of Haunted Japan: Seven Tales of Horror and the Supernatural and Tales of Filipino Terror: Ten Stories of Myth and Fear, which gained international recognition. Their works masterfully blend ancient legends with modern horror, captivating audiences worldwide. Their gripping tales dive into the darkest realms of myth and terror, mesmerizing readers from all walks of life.

Their latest book, Dark Tales of Asia: 8 Stories of Cursed Legends and Dark Myths, continues their exploration of Asian folklore, intertwining chilling legends with contemporary horrors. Their books are available on Amazon Kindle, Apple, Barnes & Noble, Hoopla, and more.

Connect with them and join their community on Facebook: facebook.com/groups/3071308739856084.

Acknowledgments

We want to express our deepest gratitude to everyone who supported the creation of this book, especially to our families for their unwavering encouragement and patience and to our friends, who have been there every step of the way. Special thanks to our readers, whose passion for folklore and horror drives us to continue exploring these dark realms. We are forever indebted to the countless legends and stories that have sparked our imaginations. Lastly, thank you to the platforms that help share our work with the world.

About the Book

Dark Tales of Asia: 8 Stories of Cursed Legends and Dark Myths takes readers on a terrifying journey into the heart of Asia's most haunted legends. In this chilling collection, Jayson R. Valencia and Rodulfo Q. Todio unravel eight eerie stories of cursed creatures, supernatural revenge, and dark magic lurking within the folklore of various Asian cultures. From the bloodthirsty Tiyanak to the shape-shifting Gumiho, these myths creep from the shadows and into your nightmares, bridging ancient superstition with modern terror.

Set against eerie backdrops like haunted forests, secluded villages, and mysterious cities, each story plunges readers into a world where the boundaries between the living and the supernatural dissolve. With suspense building at every turn, Dark Tales of Asia ensures an immersive and spine-chilling experience for horror enthusiasts and fans of folklore alike.

Available on Amazon Kindle, Apple, Barnes & Noble, Hoopla, and other platforms, this collection invites readers to confront the darkness hiding in the forgotten corners of Asia. Prepare yourself for a nightmarish journey into the unknown, where every legend has a dark, sinister truth waiting to be discovered.

Thank You!

Thank you for diving into Dark Tales of Asia: 8 Stories of Cursed Legends and Dark Myths. If you enjoyed these stories, please follow our Facebook page to learn about our latest releases, special offers, and exclusive content. Your support helps us continue bringing these thrilling tales to life.

Delve into the shadows of Asia, where folklore whispers of ancient curses and dark myths chill the soul. In Dark Tales of Asia: 8 Stories of Cursed Legends and Dark Myths, experience the terror that lurks in the corners of forgotten villages and haunted landscapes. From the blood-soaked legends of the Tiyanak to the evil spirit of Aka Manto, each tale weaves a haunting narrative that unravels the mysteries of love, betrayal, and vengeance. These are not just stories; they are warnings that echo through the ages, reminding us that some legends refuse to fade into obscurity. Are you brave enough to turn the pages?

Written by

Jayson R. Valencia
Rodulfo Q. Todio

Also by Jayson Valencia

Tales of Haunted Japan: Seven Tales of Horror and the Supernatural
Tales of Filipino Terror: Ten Stories of Myth and Fear
Dark Tales of Asia

Also by Rodulfo Todio

Tales of Haunted Japan: Seven Tales of Horror and the Supernatural
Tales of Filipino Terror: Ten Stories of Myth and Fear
Dark Tales of Asia

Milton Keynes UK
Ingram Content Group UK Ltd.
UKHW041823201024
449814UK00001B/82

9 798227 229274